Gypsy Summer
by WILMA YEO

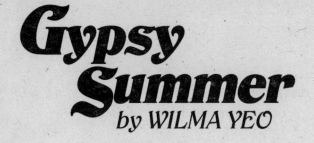

illustrated by
RICHARD WILLIAMS

SCHOLASTIC INC.
New York Toronto London Auckland Sydney

*For Marji McDonald who listened,
and for the McInnes boys, JD, Matthew and Cooper,
and for Walter, of course!*

ISBN 0-590-33756-4

Text copyright © 1986 by Wilma Yeo.
Illustrations copyright © 1986 by Scholastic Books, Inc.
All rights reserved. Published by Scholastic Inc.

12 11 10 9 8 7 6 5 4 3 2   4   6 7 8 9/8 0 1/9

Chapter

1

MY LIFE WAS already ruined even before I met Marya, the Gypsy girl. What had happened was that when school got out for the summer, every single person in the fourth grade except for me and Albert Hooper passed to fifth. I was the only girl in our room who didn't get promoted.

My mother, who was a teacher before she married my father, decided my problem was that I was a poor reader. She said I had to read fifteen books before summer vacation was over. She ended up by saying, "I know how bad you feel about this, Katy, but look at it this way: You *are* the smallest girl in your class."

"Smallest, yeah," I said, "and dumbest." My mother just shook her head and looked worried.

My little brother, Walter, who had passed from third up *to* fourth — so now we'd be in the same room — offered to help me learn to read better.

I told Walter no thank you, that what I really intended to do was run away and join the circus.

This got my mother more upset than ever, so I said real quick that I was only fooling. But, I thought to myself, maybe I really will run away before school starts again! Then I bet that old Miss Graham would be sorry for not passing me.

Since I couldn't bear to face my old friends anymore, I began to spend a lot of time with Walter. Even a little brother who could have been in *The Guinness Book of World Records* for reading the most books at his age is better company than nobody. Walter has always tried to stick to me like an iron-on patch, anyway, so he was glad for my company.

Our favorite place to go was over to the haunted house. We live at the edge of our town, Tarryville. Behind our house is Mr. Mortz's pasture. The old empty house we kids call the haunted house sat in the middle of Mr. Mortz's pasture. Over there I could almost forget there was such a thing as school.

Walter and I went to the haunted house almost every day right after breakfast. Since our mother has always worried that Walter reads *too* much, he would take something like his archery set or his binoculars. I would carry a couple of library books along. Then soon as we were out of sight we'd trade off.

One of the times Walter and I were on our way to the haunted house we found an unusual-looking toad. At the time we found our toad we hadn't even seen a Gypsy up close, let alone realized the powers they thought toads had. Walter looked our toad up in the encyclopedia. He found out it was a male, Great Plains toad. Our toad was brown with whitish stripes from top to bottom. He had little round, reddish bumps all over him that looked like jewels.

We decided we'd better keep our toad at the haunted house since our mother is sure that toads give you warts or worse. We named our pet toad Babe Ruth, after that famous baseball player, because we thought he'd be good at catching flies. As it turned out we had to catch all his food ourselves.

In no time Babe Ruth was so tame he'd hop up on my hand every time I flattened it in front of him. I got so I loved that fat, bumpy toad.

We brought some strong cardboard boxes from the men's clothing store where our father works and built our toad a cozy two-story home. Every day before we left the haunted house we carried Babe Ruth and his home up the creaky, narrow stairway to an upstairs room for safekeeping. Walter and I spent so much time over there with Babe Ruth that we knew every squeak and groan in the boards of the old house by heart. We got to feeling like the haunted house was our private property.

That's why, when High-Pockets Jackson, who is fourteen, dared me to stay by myself all night in the haunted house, I knew I *could* do it.

High-Pockets lives right next door to us. It was late one hot Monday afternoon when he made the dare. School had been out about two weeks. Walter and I were crossing the fence from Mr. Mortz's pasture into our backyard when High-Pockets yelled, "See any spooks over there today?"

I ignored him. He was in his yard throwing his baseball up against his roof and catching it in his glove. Walter went on inside our house, but I stopped to pull some scratchy cockle burrs off my jeans. When I straightened up, I saw High-Pockets coming into our yard.

"Got a little favor to ask you, Katy," he said.

Of course I knew what the favor would be, but I said, "Yeah?"

High-Pockets combed at his sun-bleached hair with his fingers. "The coach says if I expect to make the majors after I get out of school, I have to start right now practicing four hours every day," he said. "Trouble is finding somebody to pitch to me that many hours regular. Why don't you sign on steady, Katy?"

High-Pockets intends to be a Major League ball player some day even if it does mean practicing with a girl when he can't get anyone else. Mostly High-Pockets hates girls. If it wasn't for the fact that I can play baseball almost as good as he can, he'd never even bother to speak to me.

"Four hours a day? No way," I said.

"Come on, just *two* hours a day then," High-Pockets begged.

"Actually I'm pretty busy this summer," I said, hoping he hadn't noticed I didn't have anything better to do than read and hang around with Walter. But he had.

"Doing what?" he asked. "Going with Walter over to play ghost at the haunted, ha ha, house?" He slapped his baseball into his glove. "I tell you what. I dare you to go over there after dark by yourself and stay all night. If you lose the dare, you pitch to me two hours every day for one week."

"Well I'm not scared to, if that's what you think," I said. "So what if *I* win?"

"Put in your order," he said, tossing his baseball in the air.

That's when I had this great idea! The thing I dreaded most about school starting next fall — the thing I practically had nightmares about every night — was walking up to that school building, seeing the kids whose room I *used* to be in, having them see me walking with just Walter. But if I walked up with an older boy, a popular boy like High-Pockets, it would . . . well, it wouldn't be *nearly* as bad.

"Walk me to school the whole first week?" I said, trying to be cool but sounding like I was afraid I'd drop the words and break them.

I was pretty sure High-Pockets didn't know yet that I'd still be in fourth grade next year, because he hadn't teased me about it.

"Sounds dumb to me," he said, "but I won't have to any how 'cause you'll never do it."

Little did he know! I'd have stayed over there a *week* alone. But there was a small problem. I glanced toward our back screen door. "One thing," I said. "My mother would never let me stay all night at the haunted house, but I'll go so early in the morning it'll be pitch-dark. Practically night. And I'll stay till daylight."

High-Pockets agreed. I tried not to let him see how glad I was as we shook hands and spit over our left shoulders to seal the dare.

Chapter
2

WHEN I GOT out of bed the next morning, the moon and stars were still bright. I pulled on my jeans and T-shirt without turning on a light and began feeling my way down the hall toward the stairs.

Once I was safely past my mother and father's room I breathed a little easier. I wasn't worried about waking up my older brother, Ben. Ben was sixteen and as my mother says, it practically takes an act of congress to get him out of bed mornings. It was Walter I was scared might hear me. He slept in the little room at the head of the stairs.

I knew if Walter woke up he'd insist on coming with me.

Once I was safely downstairs I hurried through the house and out the back door. There weren't any lights next door where High-Pockets lived, nor at the Rayhill's on the other side of us.

Even in the dark I didn't have any trouble finding the broken-down place in the fence where Walter and I always climbed through on our way to the haunted house.

As often as we'd been over there, we never did just go straight up to the haunted house the way we would have a regular house. Just the sight of it — lonely and spooky-looking with its windows all broken out and the front door hanging by one hinge — somehow slowed us down. We'd get real quiet and sort of sneak up on the house every time . . . just in case, I guess.

Once, right after school let out, we knew someone else had been in the haunted house after we left it. We knew, because it had rained during the night, and that next morning we found muddy footprints all the way up the back door steps. Our mother heard us talking about it that night and she said, "Well, if there is ever anybody else over there, you two are to come straight back home!"

If my mother could speak six languages she'd use all six of them to worry with. Still, as I headed alone across Mr. Mortz's dark pasture it was kind of comforting to think that, even though my mother had no idea of what I was up to, she was probably worrying about me in her sleep.

Up ahead of me the old house looked lonelier than ever in the moonlight. I slowed down. Something bumped me from behind and I let out a yell.

I whirled around, then sighed with relief. It was only Walter. He was still wearing his pajamas which our mother had cut off at the knees for summer.

"Go back Walter, pl — eeze," I said.

"Nope," Walter said. Walter doesn't talk much, but he means every word he says. I decided to explain the dare to him and hope that would convince him to let me go on alone.

But when I'd finished, he just said, "*I'll* walk to school with you next fall."

"You're too young to understand," I said, knowing that wouldn't do any good. "Will you at least go back before the sun starts to come up? Promise!"

In his deep voice, which in the stillness sounded awfully loud, Walter said, "Might. Might not." I had to settle for that.

We struck out across the stubble of grass toward the shadowy shape of the haunted house. Ordinarily Walter and I went into the old house through the back doorway that didn't have a door on it anymore, so that's where I headed. But I was worrying so much about losing my dare that I stumbled and almost fell over the boarded-up well, which I had stepped across a hundred times, at the back corner of the house.

That was why Walter saw *it* before I did!

"Katy! Look!" he stammered.

I strained to see through the dark. He was pointing at the crumbly cement post we sometimes set tin cans on for archery practice. But that was no tin can sitting on the post now! I couldn't believe what I saw. It was a skull! A white skull gleaming like ivory in the moonlight.

Right at that minute I was so scared I wouldn't have let Walter go home without me if it meant the President of the United States would walk me to school. Still it wasn't the kind of scared you run from, so I crept closer to the thing. Walter was right behind me.

It was a skull sure enough, but it wasn't egg-shaped like a human skull. It was long and flat, more like the skull of an animal — a horse maybe.

I looked over at the black square where the back door of the haunted house used to be. "Let's look inside," I whispered.

We tiptoed toward the house, then crouched down and crept up the splintery steps.

What we saw, outlined by moonlight coming through the broken window, didn't make us feel any easier. In the middle of the room, which had always been empty before, sat a small, old-fashioned, three-legged black kettle with a long stick in it. Beside the kettle was an upended wooden crate with a glass jar on top.

There were more things farther back but it was too dark to tell what they were. I was sure Walter was thinking, the same as I was, that somebody could be in there right now.

It was so quiet I could hear Walter breathing. We listened a minute for any kind of noise from inside the house. When we didn't hear anything I reached for Walter's hand, and we slowly stood up together to get a better look.

The next second I let out a yelp, dropped Walter's hand, and cleared all three steps to the ground in one leap. Something had tapped me on the end of my nose!

I looked back. Walter was still standing there on the top step. "Egg," he whispered.

"W-What do you mean — *egg*?" I was shaking

like there was an earthquake going on under my feet.

"I mean, it was an egg." Walter pointed to something small hanging in the doorway.

I climbed sheepishly back up the steps beside Walter.

Sure enough, hanging by plain old thread fastened to the top of the doorway, was a small woven holder just the size for the egg inside it. This positively wasn't the kind of thing an ordinary person would do. Maybe this was all set up by High-Pockets to scare me out of the dare. But I really didn't think so. He didn't have that much imagination.

"Let's sneak around to the front and look in there," I whispered.

As we inched our way around the outside of the house the pasture grass crackled under our feet, and I thought if there *was* anyone inside they would surely hear us.

When we reached the front I motioned for Walter to stop at the first window, and I peeked in.

The two front rooms were bare as always. The same old strips of faded brown wallpaper were hanging from the walls, leaving crumbly plaster showing through in places.

I moved back from the window and shook my head. "Nothing's different here," I whispered. "Do you suppose somebody's hiding upstairs?"

Walter shrugged. He is not easily upset.

But the minute I said the word *upstairs* I remembered Babe Ruth! "You don't think anything has happened to Babe Ruth, do you?" I asked.

"Nope." It was Walter's favorite word.

I hoped he was right. Probably, I thought, whoever set up that skull and put those things in the kitchen hadn't even gone upstairs. But who could have done it? Was the skull some kind of warning?

Just then I noticed light was barely beginning to show in the eastern part of the sky, and I realized I had lost the dare with High-Pockets. The way things had turned out I couldn't even blame Walter. It's funny how daylight changes your feelings. I wasn't scared anymore. I was just plain mad. Mad at the unknown person who had taken over our house, and caused me to lose my chance to have High-Pockets walk me to school next fall.

But daylight also meant that Mother would be getting up to send our brother Ben off to work. If she discovered Walter and me missing from our beds she'd probably be so scared she'd call Sheriff Wallace.

"We better get home quick," I said. "But we'll come right back here after breakfast and settle all this with whoever moved those things into our haunted house."

Chapter
3

WHEN WE STEPPED back into our own yard it was fairly light and I was thankful at least that High-Pockets wasn't out this early. I'd have to admit soon enough that I lost the dare. I promised myself that before the summer was over I'd think of another way to get High-Pockets to make the same offer. Or maybe I'd even get some awful disease and not have to go to school at all.

Right now the big thing was I didn't want to have to start paying off before Walter and I had a chance to see about Babe Ruth and try to solve the mystery of those things at the haunted house.

I was certainly not going to tell High-Pockets about them. First thing he was bound to ask was, why hadn't Walter and I gone on inside. I could already see how he'd grin figuring *we* didn't because *I* was scared to.

Mother was already fixing breakfast. I knew she hadn't missed us because she looked surprised instead of relieved when we walked in. She must have thought we had just been in the backyard since Walter was still wearing his pajamas. She sent him to his room to dress.

To hurry things up I helped by making the toast. I decided to make it cinnamon, which is my favorite. While I was sprinkling on the cinnamon, the funniest notion came to me that I had already smelled something spicy like that this very morning. It seemed to come back to me that there had been a funny spicy smell around the doorway of the haunted house. But that's crazy, I thought. Still, it wasn't any crazier than what we'd seen over there.

Soon as we finished eating and had cleared off and rinsed our plates good enough to satisfy our mother — which is real good — we started for the haunted house again. I carried a library book this time so my mother wouldn't fuss.

As we cut across Mr. Mortz's pasture I explained my plan to Walter. "First we'll look in the back again to make sure whoever put those things inside the kitchen isn't in there," I said.

Walter nodded.

"If we don't see anyone we'll call out, 'Anybody anywhere in this house?' If nobody answers, we'll hurry around to the front, go inside, and hide upstairs in Babe Ruth's room over the kitchen."

Walter nodded again.

"We'll look down through that hole in the floor

where the boards are rotted away," I went on. "We can see whoever comes in the room below without them knowing we're watching. We'll stay until someone shows up, which they are bound to do."

By this time we were more than halfway across the pasture so we slowed up to keep an eye out for any sign of life over by the house. When we reached it we stayed close alongside and crept, quiet as we could, around to the back.

The skull was still on the post. It didn't look nearly as scary this time. Even so, I could feel my heart going about twice as fast as it should.

That dumb egg was still hanging in the doorway. Inside the kitchen everything was exactly the same as earlier, only now that it was light we saw what the other things were: an old shoe box over in one corner and some ragged, bright-colored pillows stacked in another.

Then I noticed the smell. It *was* a spicy smell, but so faint I had to breathe in and hold my breath to be sure. That homey smell, along with the rush I was in to see about Babe Ruth, gave me the courage to call out, "A-Anybody here?" There wasn't an answer so I tried again, louder this time to make sure I could be heard all the way upstairs. There still wasn't any answer. So Walter and I started around to the front of the house.

The stairway to the second floor was just inside the front door. The bottom step going upstairs had been missing for as long as we'd been coming there. When I stepped across the empty space, my weight made the next step groan like a ghost with a stomachache. I hurried on up with Walter's knees bumping against my heels all the way.

We hardly ever spent any time upstairs in the haunted house — just stayed long enough to put our toad up there. Those narrow steps were the only way back down. Even when things were normal you sort of felt cornered all the time you were up in the small, empty rooms.

We took a quick look to make sure nobody was hiding in the first two rooms and hurried on to the one right above the kitchen. When I reached the doorway I stopped dead in my tracks.

Babe Ruth's house was turned over on its side! I ran to it and looked in it, under it, and then all around the room. Babe Ruth was gone!

"Some blasted thief stole Babe Ruth!" I cried, forgetting all about being quiet.

Walter pounded his first into his palm. I knew he was as angry as I was. There was something very helpless about that toad. And something loving, too, about the way he'd sit so heavy on your hand and look at you as if he could think.

"Now we *have* to find whoever's been here," I said, mad as all get out.

I took one more look inside Babe Ruth's house, then went over to the hole in the floor. I dropped my book and stretched out on my stomach next to the hole. Walter squatted down beside me.

From up there we had a different view of those things in the room below. I saw that the glass jar had what looked like dirty water in it. On top of the beat-up shoe box was a small, brown pouch with something lumpy-looking inside it.

The longer I looked down there, the madder I got knowing that whoever those things belonged to had stolen poor, trusting Babe Ruth.

After we had waited awhile and nothing happened Walter sat up and reached for my book. I guess Walter would read during a tornado if it didn't blow his book away.

Suddenly there was a crunching of footsteps in the weeds outside the house. Walter closed the book with his finger marking his place and looked through the hole again. I held my breath hoping it wasn't High-Pockets coming to get me to pay off our dare.

A strange girl with hair black as coal came running into the kitchen. Her bare feet landed on the boards as light as a butterfly lands on a flower. Her full yellow skirt came clear to her ankles. She had on a faded red drawstring blouse. I wondered if her clothes were some kind of costume.

I nudged Walter, put my finger to my lips, then pointed down. It was a signal we'd keep still and watch until we discovered what she was up to.

The girl's skin was berry brown. I could tell her dark hair was curly even though it was pulled into two long braids. My own hair is poker straight, so I always notice curly. She was carrying a big, bulky bag with three white X's stamped on it.

I wondered if she had our toad in that bag! I hardly breathed as I watched her pull something from it. But it turned out to be only a large empty can. Then she reached in again and brought out a much smaller can. She pried off the lid with her fingers. Then she set the small can down inside the big one. She pulled a match from her pocket, struck it on the floor, and held it down inside the big can. Something flamed up with a tiny poof.

Every move the girl made was quick and sure. We watched her lift the black kettle and balance it on top of the two cans.

She took the stick that was inside the kettle and laid it on the floor. The stick had been cut from a tree and had three prongs on the end of it. She poured the jar of water into the kettle.

Next she reached into her bag again and pulled out a little paper sack. She began dropping handfuls of something that looked like corn meal into the

kettle. Each time she dropped some in she counted out loud, almost like singing, "One, two, three, four, five, six, seven."

I wondered if she could be cooking food. It sure didn't look very appetizing.

I felt as if we were watching someone on a stage. The girl planted her brown feet wide apart and dug into the pocket of her skirt again. She made every move as if she *knew* she had an audience. She brought out something that splashed like stones as she let them fall one at a time into the kettle, counting again to seven. Her voice was strong and clear.

Then she began to stir the mixture with the three-pronged stick and chant, this time in a strange, trembly voice:

"Evil eyes look on thee,

May they here extinguished be!"

Evil eyes! I shuddered and a chill like ghosts' fingers brushed against the back of my neck.

Just then the girl must have thought she heard something outside because she dropped her stirring stick and spun around toward the window. I saw a flash of something bright as she spun. She was wearing big gold loops in her ears.

Suddenly I knew. This girl had to be a Gypsy! But where did she come from?

I glanced to see how Walter was taking all this. He seemed to be as bewildered as I was. When I looked back down, the girl was starting to stir and chant again:

"Evil eyes *now* look on thee,
May they soon extinguished be!"

I began to feel almost hypnotized by her skinny brown hand going round and round, and hearing her chant filling the haunted house. I felt floaty like you do the second before you fall asleep.

She's a Gypsy all right, I decided. I had never seen one up close this way before, though a band of Gypsies in cars and trucks, some of them even pulling bright painted wagons, had passed through Tarryville last summer and the summer before that. Our mother wouldn't let us go see them, though. She's afraid of Gypsies. I was beginning to see why.

The strange girl kept on stirring and chanting, only now her voice had quit trembling, and was more excited sounding:

"Evil eyes now look on thee
May they soon extinguished be!
May they burn, may they burn,
In the fire forever!"

Just as the Gypsy girl said, "forever," Walter sneezed!

Chapter
4

WALTER AND I ducked back real fast. But it was too late.

"Who's up there?" the girl cried.

I decided then that I wasn't going to let some strange girl, who had stolen our toad and taken over our haunted house, get away with this. I peeked over the edge again. "It's me, Katy Collings," I called down in a want-to-make-something-of-it voice. "Me and my brother."

The girl stood there looking up at me, her hands on her hips. She swished her long skirt. "You get out of there," she ordered. Her eyes were black as burnt marshmallows and hot-angry as if they were still smoking.

"This is *our* house. *You* get out!" I shouted.

"I'll never!" She raised her fist at us.

"You stole our toad!" I said.

"I ain't never *cored* nothing," she screamed. "Toads are free for the taking. And this house was here empty and I found it. It's mine. I'm gonna count ten, then if you are still up there I'm gonna set fire to this here place!"

Through my mind flashed a picture of our mother running screaming toward the flaming house. I grabbed Walter's arm and pulled him to his feet. I didn't let go of him all the way down as we bumped against the narrow stairway walls. We jumped the last two steps and landed right in front of the girl.

She was waiting with her hands still on her hips. I let go of Walter's hand and gave her a good shove. "Where's my toad?" I demanded.

"Gone. That's where," she said. "Now git out of here."

I was so blasted mad, and scared that maybe Babe Ruth was dead, that I started to cry. Quick, before she could see that I was, I turned and marched out of the front door of the haunted house, trying to act like I was leaving because I wanted to.

Soon as I was sure Walter was safely outside, too, I stopped and looked back. The girl was watching us. She was leaning with one hand against the doorway and almost doubled up laughing. "Run, *gorgios,* run," she shouted at us.

Even though I didn't know what she was calling

us, I was mad as a bee shut up in a jar. "You Gypsy!" I yelled.

"Sure thing I'm a Gypsy — a Romany," she called out with her head thrown back proud-like now. "Tribe of Marks, Kalderasha strain. I am the seventh daughter of a seventh daughter. If you ever show up here again I'll put a curse on that runty brother of yours so he'll sicken and grow weaker and weaker until he dies!"

Right off another picture of our mother flashed through my mind. This time she was wringing her hands and crying at the side of poor Walter's death bed. "Let's go," I said to Walter, but loud enough for that girl to hear. "We will get Sheriff Wallace to make her give back our toad and make her stay out of our house." Of course my threat was only a trick to scare her.

But as Walter and I turned our backs and started off, she called out, "You do, and that day will be the sorriest one of your life."

I remembered how spellbound I had felt just listening to her chant about the Evil Eye, and I was scared *her* threat was more than just a trick.

Chapter
5

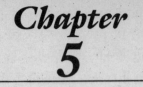

As I was crossing the fence ahead of Walter, he shocked me by saying, "If you had acted nicer to her, we might have found out where Babe Ruth was."

I stopped halfway over and stared back at him. "Acted nicer? To *her*?" I still had plenty of leftover anger in me. "What did you want me to say — 'I'm pleased to meet you?'"

Walter just shrugged. He always draws into a shell where I can't reach him when I get mad.

For the second time that morning we got inside our house without running into High-Pockets. My mother greeted me with, "Katy, right after lunch you are to take off those dirty jeans, get cleaned up, and walk downtown to Doctor Miller's office. I phoned him about the filling you lost. He said for you to come in at two."

It didn't seem fair, but I didn't argue. I was so miserable about Babe Ruth I figured I'd just as soon suffer some more.

By the time I was ready to leave for the dentist

I was really feeling sorry for myself. So before I left I said to Walter, in private, "To keep my mind off the terrible pain I will try to figure out an answer to our problem." I was hoping to make him feel sorry about what he'd said to me earlier.

"I'll think, too," he said, which I mistakenly took to mean he *was* sorry.

Doctor Miller didn't really hurt me and I felt better after that hole in my tooth was filled.

Mother was getting the mail from the box when I came up the front steps. "Where's Walter?" I asked.

"He said something about you forgetting your library book over at the pasture house this morning." My mother sighed. "I think he went to get it. You know how particular Walter is about taking care of library books, and I think it's you who should. . . ."

I had stopped listening. Walter had gone to the haunted house alone! Was that Gypsy girl still there? Maybe she had already put a curse or something on Walter! "'Scuse me!" I said over my shoulder as I shot down the front steps two at a time. I went tearing around the side of our house and into the backyard. Just as I got to the fence I heard High-Pockets yell, "Hey, Katy, what goes about our dare?"

"Tell you later," I called. I couldn't waste time explaining.

I ran straight up to the haunted house this time, jumped the old wooden well platform, and headed for the back doorway. Before I got up the steps I heard voices so I know they were both in there.

But I wasn't expecting what I saw from the doorway where the stupid egg still dangled.

Walter and the Gypsy girl were sitting cross-legged on the floor facing each other.

They both looked up at me in surprise. The Gypsy girl grabbed something out of Walter's hands and hid it with her full skirt before I could see what it was. "Git out," she said, narrowing her black eyes.

My library book was lying on the floor by Walter. "I wish you hadn't come over here, Katy," he said, and his voice sounded different to me somehow. I just stood there struck dumb. What was going on?

I dropped down on my knees beside my very own brother. "Has she already put a curse on you?" I whispered desperately. I sniffed. Walter seemed to have that same strange spicy smell about him that I'd smelled earlier.

Walter looked right past me in a very peculiar way. "I made a pact with her," he said. "She brings back Babe Ruth and I — "

"Shut up!" the girl said, leaning into Walter's face. "I don't want her knowin'!"

"I'll just bet you don't!" I yelled. "You undo whatever you've done to Walter or I'll get my father. He'll — "

"You do and I'll put a curse on him, too. Now

30

get out, both of you. And tomorrow *he* better be the only one who comes or you'll both be sorry."

I stood up and pulled Walter up after me. He reached back to get my book. The Gypsy girl didn't move. She just stared at me like she was trying to burn holes through me with those fiery dark eyes. I shoved Walter toward the back doorway. At least I knew now that Babe Ruth was alive. Or was she lying about bringing him back?

When we were almost down the back steps the girl called after us, "Remember Walter, the Evil Eye will know if you tell *her*."

She was even calling my brother by name. Soon as we were out of hearing range I said, "What did she mean? If you tell me *what*?"

"Nothing," Walter said.

I was so fighting mad I could have licked a whole tribe of Gypsies. "But you *have* to tell me. And how did she know your name?"

"I told her," Walter said. "Hers is Marya. Spelled M-a-r-y-a. You say it like Mary only with an 'a' on the end. Mary-a."

"I don't care if her name's Pickle Face," I said. "What did she mean when she said 'The Evil Eye will know' if you tell me — tell me what? And what did *you* mean about making a pact with her?"

Walter stopped and looked straight at me, then blinked a few times like he does when something is important to him, and said what was probably the longest sentence of his life up to then. "Katy, if you don't try to make Marya like you, you are going to have to stay home when I meet her every day at the haunted house."

Walter had *changed* already!

Meet her! My nose prickled like I was about to sneeze — or cry. "Walter Edward Collings," I said, grabbing hold of his shoulders, "you tell me this instant why you are going over there to meet that Gypsy girl."

"Promised her I wouldn't tell," Walter said stubbornly.

"What's gotten into you?" I yelled. "She *must* have put a spell on you. What did she do?" The truth is I was half scared he would start to "sicken and die" right there and then.

"Don't be silly," Walter said in his I-have-finished-speaking voice. Then he walked on *ahead* of me.

I knew there was no use trying to find out anything more from him. But suddenly I did remember where I could find out whether Gypsies really could put spells on people or not. Tomorrow morning would be Wednesday, the day for Walter's trombone lesson. When my mother took Walter for his lesson *I* would go visit the only person I knew who could help me — Aunt Lolly Forsythe.

Chapter
6

AUNT LOLLY ISN'T really anybody's aunt, but everyone in Tarryville calls her that. She is the only person I know who talks to kids in the same voice she uses for grown-ups. She lives alone in the big house where she was born.

Her fancy old house, covered halfway up with vines, is one block south of the Tarryville Courthouse. It was built by her father, Clement Forsythe, who was the founder of our town. On top of the third story of Aunt Lolly's house is a little tower room crowned with a spiky, black iron railing.

The tower room is filled with things that used to belong to Aunt Lolly's mama and things that belonged to Aunt Lolly when she was a child: old books, ice skates, dolls, things like that.

Aunt Lolly is too old and fat now to climb the winding stairsteps to the tiny tower room herself. Whenever she wants any of her "Mama's treasures" brought down from up there, she sends someone to fetch them.

"Run up to the tower room" she'll say to whoever is "helping her out" that day, "and fetch me Mama's little silver snuff box," or whatever it is she wants to see again, or give away.

Aunt Lolly sees to it that she is never lonely by hiring lots of "help." Only she doesn't have them work. Mostly they just sit at Aunt Lolly's kitchen table, which is covered with a pink lace cloth, and have sugar cookies and oolong tea, and a friendly visit.

I knocked on her back door right after ten o'clock on Wednesday morning.

"Come in, Dearie," Aunt Lolly called before she even knew who it was.

I had been hoping, but not expecting, to find Aunt Lolly alone for once.

Aunt Lolly knows everything about Gypsies. When her own mama was a young girl she was a close friend of the famous Gypsy fortune-teller Urania Boswell, who lived in England. But when Aunt Lolly's mama married Clement Forsythe, he told her she was never to "raggle taggle after Gypsies again." Aunt Lolly always looks sad when she tells that part.

"Mama *did* miss her Gypsy friends," Aunt Lolly will say. Then she'll look more cheerful and add proudly, "But she had me to talk to about them.

Mama talked to me about her Gypsy friends by the hour. And that is why I grew up wise in the ways of Gypsies."

Aunt Lolly herself once had a Gypsy friend named Volga. Up until about a year ago Volga had a fortune-telling place in a storefront in the city. Aunt Lolly went there by bus every Friday afternoon to see her. The storefront had thin silver curtains across the window and it sounded like a very mystic and strange place to me. Aunt Lolly told me Volga was using her powers to help trace down a diamond ring that Aunt Lolly had lost.

But then, on the very day Volga was going to reveal the exact spot where the ring was, Aunt Lolly arrived at the storefront and found it empty. Even the silver curtains were gone.

Aunt Lolly seemed to mind losing her Gypsy friend more than she minded not finding her lost diamond ring. I suppose that is because Aunt Lolly has plenty more diamond rings.

She told me one time that it was mainly on account of her dead father that she worried about losing that ring. She said, "Papa always warned me: 'Lolly, expensive jewelry is a terrible obligation!' "

She still has more jewelry than she can wear at one time. But she *always* wears her little pearl and amethyst tiara around the loose knot of hair on top of her head, because that tiara was given to Aunt Lolly's mama a long, long time ago by the famous Urania Boswell.

Aunt Lolly had the tiara on *this* morning, and it was tilted a little to one side like it always was.

I sat down at the table. Aunt Lolly heaved herself from her chair and got out another of her thin china cups for me. She poured it full of oolong tea. Then she refilled her own, not minding that she spilled some on her pink lace table cloth. Soon as Aunt Lolly sat down again I sort of eased into what I had come to find out about by asking, "Do you know what a *gorgio* is?"

Aunt Lolly adjusted her tiara. "Of course, Dearie. I can speak Romany, though not with the lovely rich accent Mama did. That has to come from living among Gypsy folk. A *gorgio* is the Gypsy word for anyone who is not a Gypsy. Most Gypsies look down on *gorgios*. Volga didn't feel that way about me, though. And *no* Gypsy felt that way about Mama."

I thought to myself, that Marya Gypsy sure feels that way about me! But I didn't have time to waste talking about how Gypsies felt. I had to find out what they could or couldn't *do*. Walter's lesson only lasted half an hour, and I had to get home before he and Mama did or else have her ask me why I had gone to see Aunt Lolly.

So I took the sugar cookie Aunt Lolly was holding out to me and said, "Is it really true that Gypsies have the power to put spells on people?" My heart pounded just from knowing I was going to find out the truth one way or the other.

I hoped for, but didn't expect, a straight out answer because Aunt Lolly loves to talk on the subject of Gypsies.

"That depends on lots of things," she began, which right away made the worry place inside me draw into a tight knot. "Gypsies are blessed with a deep insight — a sort of *seeing* the rest of us don't have. By treasuring and using this blessing all down through the generations they have made it even stronger, Katy."

I took a long breath. I still didn't know if Walter was in some kind of danger or not. I tried again. "But *can* they cast spells on people?"

"You take a Gypsy *dukkerer,* she's a fortune-teller," Aunt Lolly said. "She can tell what *has* happened and what is going to happen, but she can't *make* things happen. But you take a *shaman,* that's a Gypsy woman who knows all about good or evil spirits. She can cast spells or remove them. To be a *shaman* a Gypsy has to be either born with a veil over the forehead, which proves she has the

'gift,' or be the seventh daughter of a seventh daughter."

I gasped. That was exactly what Marya had said she was! The worry knot in my chest came right up into my throat. "Gotta go," I said, jumping up.

"Wait." Aunt Lolly looked up at me, her green-gold eyes sparkly with hope. "Are there Gypsies in town?"

I hesitated. Since that Gypsy girl Marya was here, there were surely more Gypsies around somewhere. But if I started telling Aunt Lolly about Marya I'd never get home ahead of Walter and my mother. Still I knew Aunt Lolly was always eager to find Gypsies to talk with. I supposed she even hoped one of them might be her friend, Volga, who could help her find her lost diamond. "I'm not sure," I said at last. "I'll come back and tell you if I find out more about it."

"Promise?" Aunt Lolly asked, and I nodded. Aunt Lolly beamed. "There's a good girl, Dearie," she said.

I said good-bye, then I hurried out the back door.

In the short time I'd been inside Aunt Lolly's kitchen, dark clouds had closed in Tarryville so that it seemed even hotter. The clouds mumbled around up there, as if they were as undecided about whether or not to rain as I was about whether or not I had better tell my mother about the Gypsy girl threatening to put a spell on Walter.

Of course Aunt Lolly had said that Gypsies could also take spells away. And Walter himself, even though he was acting very strangely, had said don't be silly when I asked him if Marya had already put a spell on him. And she *had* said she would give back our toad if Walter . . . If Walter did what? I wondered miserably.

39

Chapter 7

MY MOTHER AND Walter did get home ahead of me, but only Mother was in the kitchen. "Where's Walter?" I asked before she even had time to ask where I'd been. I was panting and puffing because of running all the way from Aunt Lolly's, and my words sounded as if my throat was rusty.

My mother, who was stirring something on the stove, turned and looked at me the way she does when she thinks I might have a fever. But all she said was, "Up in his room."

I breathed easier.

My mother went back to stirring. "He's reading, I suppose," she added over her shoulder. "That boy! He already knows more than he should for his age."

I wondered what would happen if I told her that reading too much might be nothing compared to what *could* happen to Walter. What could *already* have happened.

My mother was making dried beef gravy, which I usually love. Today I didn't feel hungry even for dried beef gravy on hot buttered toast.

There would only be the three of us for lunch because my brother Ben packs a lunch in summer. He makes good money stripping blue grass with three of his friends. They sell the seeds to the man who owns the Feed 'N' Seed store in Tarryville. I thought now, maybe I would ask Ben tonight, sort of off-handedly, if he had seen any Gypsy camps around when he was out working. Maybe I could find out if it looked as if they were going to camp here for long.

My mother handed me the jar of sweet pickles, which I usually consider to be delicious with dried beef gravy. I put them on the table. Then I told her I'd go up and tell Walter lunch was ready. When you are worried about someone having a spell on them, you feel better if that person is in sight.

Walter's door was shut so I knocked, which our mother insists we do.

"What?" Walter answered.

"Can I come in?"

"No."

"What are you doing?" I asked.

"Coming out."

I opened his door a crack and looked in. Walter jumped back from his bed, but in that split second I saw him hide something under his mattress. He had never kept a secret from me before and now here was the second one since that Gypsy had come into our life. The first, of course, being about the pact he'd made with her.

I pretended I hadn't noticed he was doing anything unusual. But I planned to come back later and find out what he'd hidden from me. "Lunch is ready," was all I said, and walked away.

When we'd finished eating, Walter and I rinsed the dishes as usual, but I didn't speak to him. Then he said he was going for a bike ride.

Since he knew my bike had flats, that meant he didn't want me along. And anyway Walter hates things like bike riding. He was not acting like himself at all. I wished I had taken the time to ask Aunt Lolly what the first signs of a spell were.

My mother was plainly pleased that Walter was going to do something besides read. "Good," she said, "but it looks like rain, so don't go too far."

I couldn't help thinking that my mother wouldn't have been so pleased if she'd known Walter's plan for later in the afternoon. I'd have told her right then and there except I knew that would mean we'd never see poor Babe Ruth again.

At least with Walter gone I'd have a chance to see what was under his mattress. I watched from the window until he rode around the corner, then I dashed upstairs.

I lifted Walter's mattress on the side he'd been standing on. Nothing. I rolled the mattress farther back and searched that whole side. Then the other. But whatever Walter had been hiding was gone now. It is a strange feeling to have your very own brother, who has always stuck to you like gum to a shoe, turn against you.

Just then, through Walter's open window I heard High-Pockets yell my name. That gave me an idea. I'd go play ball in High-Pockets' backyard. That way I'd be sure to see Walter later as he left for the haunted house to meet Marya alone. "Coming," I yelled back.

My plan was to let Walter get a head start, then when he'd gone inside the haunted house, I'd follow him and listen from outside.

Even the clouds, which were getting darker now, were in my favor. I could use them for an excuse to quit playing ball whenever I needed to.

High-Pockets was waiting in his yard. "I guess you got scared out of the dare huh?," he said, grinning.

Partly because it was true and partly to please him, I said, "Guess so."

"Remember, two hours," he said tossing one glove at me.

I made a big thing of checking on the sky. "Okay,

but my mother gets worried if the clouds look too bad."

"She afraid your hair will uncurl if it gets wet?" he asked.

Since my hair doesn't even bend, let alone curl, I ignored that. High-Pockets doesn't have a mother, only a father, so I sort of understand why he talks that way.

He stung one into my glove and I stung one right back. If I wasn't a girl I figure I'd have as much chance of getting into the Major Leagues as High-Pockets because of all the practicing I've done with him. Maybe by the time I'm old enough that rule will be changed. Then I bet everyone will forget I didn't pass fourth grade.

We'd been playing about half an hour when Walter marched out our back door and without even glancing in my direction trotted off across the pasture. He was carrying something in a flat paper sack like the kind greeting cards come in.

I pretended not to see him, but it upset me even more than I had expected — to actually see him going off to meet that girl without me. I was so put out at Walter that I threw the ball a mile wide and High-Pockets said a word my mother won't let me even think!

While High-Pockets chased the ball I kept track

of Walter as long as I could. I figured to wait about three more minutes before I gave High-Pockets my fake excuse for quitting.

As it turned out, more than the weather cooperated because just as I caught the next ball my older brother, Ben, came out our back door and called, "Hey, High-Pockets, how about a game of pepper?"

Normally Ben wouldn't have been home this early, but because of lightning our mother has made him promise to quit working out in the field when it looks like rain.

High-Pockets practically snatched the glove off my hand, he was so eager to take Ben up on his unexpected offer. Little did he know I was just as glad to leave right then.

While I was crossing the fence High-Pockets called, "Remember I still have time coming, Katy." I didn't want to take a chance on my answer being heard all the way to the haunted house, so I turned with a make-believe smile on my face to let him know I understood.

Also, just in case Walter or the girl might look out and see me, I didn't head straight for the old house, but sort of meandered across the pasture pretending I'd only come to Mr. Mortz's pasture to pick a bouquet of the daisy fleabane, which was starting to bloom all over the place.

I was clutching a whole wad of those smelly little white flowers by the time I reached the haunted house. As I crept toward the back doorway I glanced at the skull on the post. By now I'd figured out that Gypsy girl had put it up to scare us away. Well it hadn't worked!

I could hear voices coming from inside the house. I squatted out of sight alongside the back steps. I held my breath so I could hear better. I don't know just what I expected to hear, but it certainly was not what I heard!

Chapter

THE GYPSY GIRL was saying, "I have to make sure of your word, that you will come here to do this every day until it is finished. After all, you are a *gorgio* — not to be trusted."

I grabbed the edge of the step and raised up a little, trying not to miss a word but still staying out of sight.

"But *you* promised to bring back our toad," Walter said. "You didn't do it."

"I'll bring him," the girl said. "I'll bring him on the day we finish."

"Nope. Tomorrow," Walter insisted.

"My father the *Rom Baro* would kill you if he knew about this — that I was meeting you here and for this reason. He is the big man, the king, the *Rom Baro!* Let me keep the toad or I'll tell him."

I almost gasped out loud. But Walter dug in his heels. "Nope," he said. "It's bring back the toad or no go. A bargain's a bargain."

Good for you, Walter, I cheered silently from my hiding place.

"That's for sure a lucky toad," the girl said in a wheedling voice. "He has seven spots on his belly. I'll pay you money for him."

"Nope."

"I have much money," the girl went on begging. "In the city, when my father went to sell earrings, I went along and told fortunes. With this lucky toad I could do even better with my *dukkerin* and get you more."

"We made a pact," Walter said. "The toad. Tomorrow!"

"As you say then," the Gypsy girl said grudgingly. "Tomorrow I'll bring him." I heard a rustling and then the girl said, "I hide it here from my father. He'd call it *gorgio* trash and likely beat me."

I gasped, but evidently they didn't hear me because Walter was saying, "Beat you? Bad?"

The girl only laughed. "No," she said, "the eagle knows the size of the wren. Here it is."

I let out my breath as quietly as I could. I desperately wanted to raise up, have a look at whatever it was she was talking about. My nose itched from the dusty weeds around me, and my legs ached from being bent so long. But I knew if I gave away my hiding place I'd never find out what was really going on in there.

I heard Walter ask, "Where'd you get it?"

"I didn't steal it," the girl said, just as if he'd accused her of that. "It was just there for the taking," she went on. "Thrown away." There was a little silence. I really had to strain to hear what she said next. "Two of my friends have fathers who are beginning to give in to some of your *gorgio* ways," she said. "These girls have been in your schools. They make fun of me when I ask what is inside your books. Now you will let me in on their secrets. See, the pictures look so very interesting."

"That's Heidi and the goats," Walter said.

Pictures! Heidi! Her secret possession must be nothing but a book! But why would she want Walter to read — Suddenly I knew. This girl, who was surely as old as I was, could not read! All she wanted of Walter was for him to read some book to her. I almost giggled I was so pleased. At least *I* could read even if I didn't like to. Then I heard Walter say, "First I made this for you."

"What is it?" the girl asked.

"A bookmark. Leather. I burned your name into it. Used my Cappers wood-burning set. See: M-a-r-y-a."

So that is what Walter had hidden under his mattress, I thought.

It was real quiet for a minute. Then the Gypsy girl said so low I could hardly hear, "My name! You are a good person — for a *gorgio*."

She was beginning to *like* Walter! Suddenly I couldn't stand it any longer. Still clutching that bunch of weeds, I jumped up, marched up the steps, ducked the egg in the doorway and announced, "Our mother wants you at home, Walter. Now. It's going to storm."

"*Carranza!*" the girl cried, leaping up from the floor and trying to hide a ragged-looking book behind her. "Don't tell," she begged Walter.

"I already know," I said. "You can't read!"

"You been spying again," the Gypsy girl yelled, stamping her foot. "*Gorgio* ways!" For the first time I noticed a tiny blue tattoo in the shape of a triangle on her cheek. "*Gorgio!*" she repeated.

This time I knew what she was calling me — a non-Gypsy. Well that suited me fine. "That's right!" I yelled back. "I am a *gorgio*. Name of Katy Collings. American." I was pleased with the way my words rang through the haunted house.

"I'm American as you," she hollered back at me. "And as for your brother, I am going to turn him into a True Rye!"

True Rye! It sounded like part of a spell! Before I had a chance to think about *that* she hollered, "Now get out! And don't come back to spy on me and Walter ever again."

Me and Walter! Who did she think she was —
practically stealing my own brother. I grabbed
Walter's hand and began pulling him toward the
back door. It was like pulling a sack of wet cement.

The Gypsy girl whirled around and snatched
Walter's other hand. "We'll read tomorrow then,"
she said. She looked at me with her dark eyes
flashing. "And if you want to ever see that toad
again, Walter better be here alone."

Walter jerked both his hands free. "I will be,"
he said calmly.

I was so mad I smashed the wilted bunch of
daisy fleabane right in Walter's face and marched
out the door.

I heard footsteps behind me and glanced back.
It was Walter. I didn't say a word to him until we
reached our fence. Then I stopped and said, "You
are certainly not going back to the haunted house
again until she's out of there."

"Have to," Walter said. "Promised. Anyway,
what about Babe Ruth?" He stood there looking at
me with one of the smashed fleabane petals still
stuck to his eyebrow.

"There are ways of getting stolen property back
from thieves," I said bitterly as I thought of how
understanding and wise our poor, kidnapped Babe
Ruth was. "Gypsy thieves especially," I added, "who

don't even know how to read."

"Now, Katy, don't — "

"Walter Edward Collings," I interrupted him, "don't you *dare* tell me again I should have been nicer to her."

"You should have," Walter said.

"She *has* put a spell on you," I sputtered. I felt like I had for sure lost the last friend I had to my name.

Walter blinked at me so I knew he was going to say something he thought was really important. The white petal fell off his eyebrow. "Tomorrow," he said, "I am going to tell Marya you are sorry."

"Like Helen of Troy you will!" I yelled.

Walter turned and deliberately started on over the fence ahead of me. "Going to," he said over his shoulder.

I knew by the way he said "going to" that he *was* going to and not even a ten-ton crane would budge him. Me, sorry? Ha! If he told her *that*, I would soon set her straight. I watched Walter go on into the house. The old Walter would have looked back to see whether I was coming or not.

When I got over into our yard I noticed High-Pockets was out in his yard alone again, throwing a baseball against the roof. Because throwing some-thing — anything — was exactly what I felt like doing, I called, "Want to play some more catch now?"

"It's about time," High-Pockets called back.

The first ball I threw whammed into his glove so hard it almost caught him off guard. He looked at me as if he really saw me for once. What he didn't know was, I was pretending his glove was that Gypsy girl's head.

By the time my mother called me to supper I felt better. The air had gotten cooler even though it hadn't rained, and I had a plan. I would let Walter go ahead and tell the Gypsy girl I was sorry. I'd even pretend it was true. Anybody so dumb they couldn't read wouldn't be hard to fool, I thought. I'd keep up the game until we got Babe Ruth back and I found out for sure whether Walter had a spell on him or not.

Besides that, I decided as an afterthought, I'll take out the thickest, hardest library book I can find, and I'll sit there reading it while she's being read *to*! As I decided this last part a squiggly little question mark lit up in my mind. Katy Collings, it seemed to ask, are you jealous of that girl? I snapped my mind off to dark again. "Not even of her curly hair," I muttered.

Chapter 9

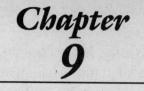

THAT NIGHT WHEN I knew Walter was alone in his room I went up and knocked on his door. He said to come in. He was reading from the encyclopedia that goes from *Ga* through *Gy*.

Right off I said, "You can go ahead and tell that Gypsy girl I'm sorry." Then, because I knew that even though she might be easy to fool, Walter wasn't, I added, "I'm not saying I like her, but I'll be nice to her if she'll be nice to me."

Walter didn't look up from the book. "You should use her name. I *told* you it's Marya," he said.

Walter had never talked to me like that before. He was under her spell all right. It seemed more important than ever that I stick by him. I said, "Okay, you can tell Marya tomorrow that I'm sorry."

Walter glanced up, then looked back down. "Good. I'll let you know what she says."

I pictured myself the next day sitting on our back steps waiting for Walter to bring me permission from Marya the Gypsy queen to enter *my* haunted house! I figured I'd better get out of his room before I said what I really thought.

The next morning it was Walter's turn to go to the dentist, but probably just to get his usual "no cavities" report.

While Walter was gone I went to the library. Because my mother was determined that I read those fifteen books, I'd been checking out the thinnest ones. The librarian, who probably knew I didn't pass fourth grade, looked surprised when I handed her my one thick book.

At two o'clock that afternoon it was just like I'd pictured it: me sitting alone on the back steps with my book, and Walter going off to the haunted house. I thought, miserably, just a few days ago he would have preferred my company to anyone else's in the world. It was scary to see how much Walter had changed already.

I hoped High-Pockets wouldn't see me sitting there, even though I had already put in my two hours time with him earlier. I also hoped my mother wouldn't notice me and ask why I hadn't gone with Walter. In case she did notice me, I opened the thick book and pretended to read. Finally I saw Walter heading back my way.

He came up puffing a little in the wind. "She says there's a condition," he said.

"What's that?" I asked suspiciously.

"It's a Gypsy custom," Walter said. "You have to bring her an amulet. Something *found* and *white*. Can be a scrap of white cloth or ribbon. When you raise it off the ground make a wish for her. White amulet means 'peace between enemies.' Red amulet means 'friends forever,' so she says *don't* bring red."

Even the new way Walter had of talking in longer sentences proved he was under that Marya's spell.

"Who does she think she — " I began. "Did she bring Babe Ruth back?"

"Not yet," Walter admitted. "But she has a reason."

"Yeah?"

"See, Katy," Walter said looking down at his tennis shoes, "she puts him in a wire cage and at night sets him out in the *dingle* — that's an area where all the Gypsies do their cooking. Hopes he'll attract another lucky toad. If it doesn't work in three more nights she'll bring him back."

I stood up beside Walter just to remind him I was taller and older than he was. "Don't you have any feelings at all for that poor toad?" I demanded. "He's used to living in a house!"

For a second I thought Walter was getting his face screwed up to cry, but all he was doing was getting ready to sneeze, which he did three times. I might have known — Walter never cried. "The *dingle* has canvas over the top so the rain won't put out the fire," he said after he finished sneezing.

"He's probably already dead," I shouted.

"You going to do it?" Walter asked.

"No," I yelled, "I'm not. Get Babe Ruth back yourself . . . if you can."

Walter sneezed again, then said, "I better go," just as if I wasn't important enough to argue with.

"By all means, don't keep Her Highness waiting," I said.

"She really is," Walter said.

"Is what?" I asked, trying now to sound bored with the whole Gypsy business.

"Highness," Walter said. "Her mother's Queen Millie Rose. Her father's the *Rom Baro* of the whole tribe — the king!"

"I'll bet," I said.

"It's true," Walter said, looking exactly like someone under a spell. Then he turned and walked back toward the fence.

I dashed into the garage and got out Walter's bike. I rode as fast as I could around our block three times trying to get myself calmed down so I could think of a plan to rescue Walter. But the bike ride didn't help.

A couple of hours later I was sitting at the kitchen table pretending to read that darned book but really thinking, when Walter came in the back door. I tried not to let him see I was watching for any new signs that he had changed.

He began setting out things to make a peanut butter-and-jelly sandwich. That was normal enough. While he spread the peanut butter he hummed to himself in his usual maddening way, which sounds like a buzz saw a long way off. If there's one thing Walter can't do — and there probably *is* only one thing — it's carry a tune.

When his sandwich was made he took one bite out of it then carried the rest on his palm, over to the table. He sat down across from me. "Have you changed your mind?" he asked.

I tried to look surprised, as if I hadn't noticed he was there before. Up close like that I saw that Walter's eyes looked red. I wondered if that was part of the spell. "Changed your mind?" he repeated.

"No, and I'm not going to," I snapped. I was dying to add, Not unless you'll say you *need* me to help you get our toad back so I'll know you're on my side and not hers. But my pride wouldn't let me. Instead I said, "Chew with your mouth shut. You look sickening."

Walter got up and left to go sit on the back

steps. That made me feel even worse. A few days ago he would have looked hurt if I'd said that, but he'd have chewed the way I told him to. There isn't going to be anybody left in this world who likes me, I thought.

Even though they'd never say so, I was pretty sure my mother and father didn't feel the same about me since I didn't pass. The kids in my room at school probably all thought I was dumb and I didn't blame them. The only thing High-Pockets liked about me was my throwing arm. Mostly, though, I felt bad because of Walter, who had been my closest friend ever since school got out.

It's all that Marya's fault, I thought angrily. It's *her* that should bring *me* a peace offering. I'll make a wish for her all right. I wish she would disappear forever!

All the next day I moped around feeling sorry for myself and half mad at everyone — mostly Walter. I even put in extra time playing ball with High-Pockets and I rode Walter's bike around some. But no matter what I was doing I was miserable.

In the afternoon I saw Walter go off to the haunted house by himself. He came back a couple of hours later all wrapped up in his smug secret. My mother didn't seem to notice I hadn't gone to the haunted house with him. It was her turn to have bridge club next and she was busy cleaning closets and things.

In fact she was so tired that we were just having leftovers at the kitchen table. My mother and father, Walter, Ben, and I had just finished passing the cold chicken when my father startled me by saying, "Big news downtown is about a band of Gypsies camping in Walnut Grove. Seems one of them — claims to be their queen, called Queen Millie Rose — anyway she's been accused of swindling Mrs. Winterset out of some money. Sheriff Wallace has the Gypsy woman in jail. I heard she eats with the sheriff's family."

I felt my eyes bug. Marya's mother? Maybe she really was a queen after all! But in jail? I looked at Walter. He was staring at the piece of chicken in his hand as if he'd just discovered it still had all its feathers. His cheeks were puffing out like pink balloons filling with air. Suddenly what was building inside him burst out. "That's not true!"

It was almost as bad as if he had called our father a liar! The room exploded into silence.

"Explain yourself, Son," our father said, laying his fork down as carefully as if it were made out of glass.

Walter's eyebrows pointed up where they almost met in the middle. "Been reading about Gypsies," he said, which I knew at least was the truth. "They don't feel the same way about money as we do. Gypsies believe money is like air — it belongs to everyone. In a way they're right. Nobody keeps money; it circulates around."

I stared at Walter. Not even Ben had ever talked to our father like that. I was sure the spell caused it.

Our father is almost as stubborn as Walter. "Taking money under false pretenses is still stealing!" he said.

Walter wasn't giving up. "Gypsies believe if you don't think enough of your money to hold onto it no matter what, then you deserve to lose it. Their word for it is *hokanni baro*. That's Rom language and it means 'the big haul.' To Gypsies, *hokanni baro* is just good business." He looked solemnly round the table, skipping me.

Our mother looked at our father as if to say, You see, I told you he reads too much.

Of course I was pretty sure Walter hadn't read all that, that he'd gotten most of it straight from a Gypsy herself — Marya, to be exact. Marya's spell was working all right! Should I tell my parents now before it was too late?

I looked at Walter to make sure he wasn't signaling me to help him out. He was still ignoring me. "How long will she be in jail?" I asked almost in a whisper.

Our father glanced at Walter, then answered my question in a stern, but not angry voice, "Until her family raises enough money to pay her fine and pay back Mrs. Winterset."

"Oh," I said, looking down at the chicken on my plate. It could take a long time to raise money selling earrings and telling fortunes.

Walter had picked up his piece of chicken and was starting to eat again. I could tell that nothing our father had said had changed his way of thinking.

I might as well have vanished for all Walter cares anymore, I thought. So let him handle this whole mess himself — spell and all. I had never felt so miserable and mixed up in my whole life.

Chapter
10

BY THE NEXT morning I had decided I would forget all about Marya, Babe Ruth, *and* Walter and his spell. I planned to do this by really concentrating on getting into the Major Leagues someday myself — in case they did finally allow girls.

But something happened about noon that changed everything.

Walter came out of his bedroom where he'd been reading, stood at the top of the stairs, and announced in a loud voice, "I can't see!"

Our mother went running to him with me right behind her. She let out a scream when she saw Walter's face. She rushed him straight back into his room and yelled at me to stay with him while she called Doctor Harold. My knees felt like they were fastened with loose hinges as I dashed on into his room. I knew of course what was wrong with Walter. Marya's spell! Would he sicken and die fast or have a slow, lingering death?

Both Walter's eyes were swollen completely shut.

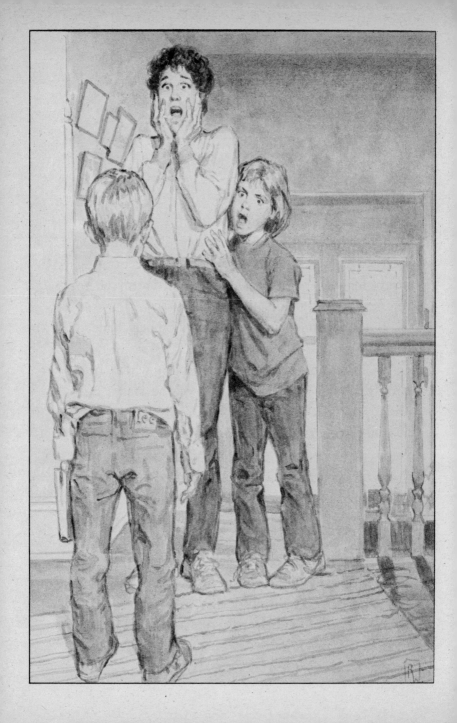

He looked awful, like he had two fat donuts where his eyes should be.

I felt a little better when Walter told me he hadn't gone blind, but just couldn't see because of the swelling. "Just when I was getting to the good part of my book, too," he added.

The doctor told our mother to drive Walter in to his office right away. Doctor Harold's office is in the city, so I knew they'd be gone at least a couple of hours. I also knew what I had to do while they were gone.

The minute their car pulled out of the driveway I headed for Aunt Lolly's. This time I'd tell her about the spell.

Even before I knocked on her back door I could hear that she had someone inside helping her out.

"Come in, Dearie," she called out.

When I got in the kitchen I saw that Joe Toggle was there talking to Aunt Lolly. Joe Toggle only has one leg, and he teases us kids by telling us that when he was young a one-legged pirate, who was jealous because Joe Toggle had two legs, cut off the other one. We really know he lost his leg in an accident back when he worked for the railroad.

Now he said, "Hi there, Katy. Found any buried treasure this summer?"

I knew he was only joking as usual, so I said, "No, not much," joking, too, of course, even though

I wasn't feeling like it. Then I sat down to drink the oolong tea Aunt Lolly had poured for me, and to wait until they finished talking.

After Joe Toggle finally left, Aunt Lolly poured more tea, passed me a sugar cookie, and said, "Now Dearie, you look worried."

"There *are* Gypsies in town," I said. "They are camping in Walnut Grove. And that's why I'm worried." I was relieved to have the subject out in the open. I started telling her about Walter and me finding Marya's things and then Marya herself in our haunted house.

Aunt Lolly listened politely with her head tilted to one side so that her pearl and amethyst tiera seemed dangerously near falling. "And now she wants Walter to read her old Heidi book to her because she's so dumb she can't even read," I said. Aunt Lolly interrupted me by raising her hand.

"But Dearie, she can't read only because that is the way of her people," she said. "And her people's people before *them*. Being a Gypsy, there are many things she *does* know. The great mystery that all people sense, but don't understand, you know, is a common, everyday part of the Gypsies' life. This is so, because they live in freedom and near to nature."

I felt like I was being betrayed by Aunt Lolly. She was making Marya sound like an awfully important person.

She went on. "Spirits whisper to us all, in our dreams, but only the Gypsy listens. He knows that truth is everywhere and that even lies lead to it."

Somehow I had to convince Aunt Lolly to be on my side. "She stole our pet toad, and she even told me she was going to turn Walter into a . . . a True Rye — whatever that means," I said, giving my tea cup an angry little shove so that it scrunched up the pink lace cloth.

Aunt Lolly chuckled. "Why, I'm a True Rye myself," she said. "That only means a person who truly loves and understands Gypsies."

I didn't even want *that* to happen to Walter! Finally I burst out with my real reason for coming here. "But because she hates *me,* she threatened to put a spell on Walter until he sickened and died! And now she's done it!"

Aunt Lolly was silent for a minute. Then she said quietly, "Be her friend, Dearie. It's the best way. Gypsies are proud people. It's best not to cross them."

It seemed to me that Marya had been the one who did the crossing: taking over our haunted house, taking over my very own brother. But all I said was, "She doesn't want *me* for a friend."

Then Aunt Lolly said, "I'll tell you what, Dearie. You send this Marya to me. Maybe I can change the way she feels about you as I've been trying to change the way you feel about her. I understand Gypsy spells and charms. I'll see what I can do. Why, I could even pay her to help me out by helping me brush up on my Romany." Aunt Lolly tilted her head the other way as she went on, "I'm losing my accent now that I don't have Volga to practice with." Then suddenly her eyes sparkled. "Perhaps she can even help me find my lost diamond ring."

I knew that if Marya helped Aunt Lolly find her ring she would for sure become Aunt Lolly's friend. I'd not only have lost Walter, but Aunt Lolly, too.

I already knew it was true what Aunt Lolly said about *her* being a True Rye. I was sure that if Aunt Lolly hadn't been so old and fat she would have raggle taggled after Gypsies like her mama. I made one last, desperate try. "Do *you* think she has cast a spell on Walter?"

Aunt Lolly patted my hand where it lay on the pink lace cloth with my uneaten cookie still in it. She looked me straight in the eye. "*If* she can cast a spell, she can take it off," she said.

That did it! Aunt Lolly's words really scared me. I could see that it was necessary for me to make peace with Marya any way I could.

I thanked Aunt Lolly for the tea and for offering to help me. After I'd told her good-bye and thanks again, I hurried out her back door.

Chapter
11

WHEN I GOT to our house I didn't even go inside. I went straight to High-Pockets' backyard. I knew exactly where I could find a scrap of white cloth. I hoped it would still be white enough to suit Marya. I climbed the big elm tree where my kite had been stuck since March. I shook the limb until the kite fell to the ground.

It had a tail torn from one of our mother's old white sheets. I tore off a piece a few inches long. Then just in case it might not work unless it was done exactly the way Walter had said, as I lifted it from the ground I made a wish for Marya. I wished that her powers to take away spells would work fast!

With my heart ticking like a time bomb I hurried toward the haunted house to meet Marya.

When I rounded the back corner of the old house I saw her standing in the doorway. She was wearing a long red dress with tiny yellow and blue flowers all over it. The sleeves were full and gathered in like a clown's ruffle at her skinny wrists. Her brown feet were bare as usual.

When she saw it was me instead of Walter, her hands flew to her hips again. I knew by now that meant she was mad. "What do you want?" she demanded.

I couldn't help thinking, I want you out of our haunted house, but I hid the way I felt. What I really wanted most was to get Walter's spell off as soon as possible. Also I didn't want her putting a spell on me, too.

I held out the dirty scrap of white cloth. "Walter said if I brought you this it would mean . . . well, it would mean you and I would . . . sort of like each other . . . I guess."

"It doesn't," Marya said, still blocking the doorway. "I am a *Rom*!" As she said that she pounded her fist on her chest. Then to impress me I guess, she said it again in what I supposed was Gypsy language, which made me all the madder. "*Rom Sam!*" Pound, pound. "You are nothing but a *gorgio*," she went on. "Not even a True Rye like your brother is to become. Where is he?"

"He doesn't feel so good," I said as calmly as I could. Choking back my real feeling I held out the scrap again. "What *does* it mean anyway, when you bring this to someone?"

"Found?" she asked, looking at me shrewdly. She hadn't budged from her spot in the doorway.

"Found," I said from the top step. "And I made a wish for you, too."

"*If* I took it, it would mean peace between enemies," she said tossing her braids. "But I ain't taking it."

"I'll make a deal with you. If you'll take this, I'll read your book out loud every day 'til Walter can come back." I prayed she really did want to hear that book as badly as she'd made Walter believe she did.

Right away I could see I had hit her in a real wanting spot because her black eyes lit up even though she kept her lips straight as a dart. "You read as good as Walter?" she asked, narrowing her eyes.

She was determined to make me show I was mad. "No I don't," I admitted. "But I *can* at least read!"

For a flicker of a second I saw I had actually hurt her pride by saying that. I almost wished it back. But then she tossed her head again. "Gypsies learn from their own people," she said haughtily. "My father, the *Rom Baro,* doesn't believe in *gorgio* schools. Says I would learn more bad than good."

I thought of the day Albert Hooper set the

wastebasket on fire so our substitute teacher wouldn't give us the test we were supposed to take. But I centainly wasn't going to admit I thought her father might be right. "Well?" I said.

"You said deal," she answered, eyeing me from the doorway like a wary sparrow. "What's in it for you?"

"I want you to go see a friend of mine, Aunt Lolly Forsythe," I blurted out. "First thing tomorrow. Please. She's already a True Rye. She'll pay you to help her out. All you have to do is talk Gypsy language with her. And maybe help her find her lost diamond ring."

"*Carranza!*" Marya said under her breath. For a second I was scared she was going to say she wouldn't go. But instead she grinned and said, "As you say then."

I had finally won a word battle with her. An important one, too, since I was almost sure Aunt Lolly would be able to change the way Marya felt about me. But then I had a thought. "You better not be lying," I said.

"May I go home to my father dead at this very moment if I am lying," she answered.

Just as I started to breathe easy again she said, "Finding lost diamond rings takes luck. I'll need to hold onto that lucky toad for a while longer."

For a split-of-a-hair second I weighed the importance of Babe Ruth against the importance of Walter. Of course Walter came out ahead. I nodded and handed her the scrap of cloth.

Marya turned and went inside. I ducked the egg hanging in the doorway and followed her. The kitchen of the haunted house looked even stranger today. Marya had tacked up a worn tapestry to two walls so that it hid that corner. Pinned to the tapestry curtain was a sign that said, "Fortunes Read." In front of the tapestry the wooden box laid flat. On it were two half-burned candles in holders made of dried mud. There were seven snail shells laid in a circle around both candle holders. The stuff she'd mixed in the black pot had dried in the bottom of it. It gave off more of that strong, spicy smell.

Marya took a match from her bag with the three X's on it and struck it on the wooden floor. She lit the two candles. Then she pinched some of the dried powdery stuff out of the black kettle and sprinkled it over the scrap of cloth. "This powder and my seven lucky snail shells will keep the Evil Eye away," she said in that same mysterious voice she'd used the first morning we saw her below us.

She sat on the floor behind the wooden box and motioned me to sit on the other side of it. She picked up the scrap of white cloth from the wooden box, turned one hand palm up and carefully placed the scrap on it. Ignoring me, she began chanting:

"One-ery, two-ery, ickery, an,
One-ery, two-ery, three.
I've seen you where you never were,
And never more shall be!"

I watched, fascinated. The candles cast a glow like a halo around her head. In the candle light she looked beautiful with her thick dark eyelashes against her cheeks and her hair curling in spidery wisps around her face. I felt like I was in another world as the spicy smell filled the air around us and mixed with the sweet, hot smell of the burning candles. I thought of what Marya had said about the spicy powder. Was the Evil Eye here in our haunted house? Was it watching us now?

I watched Marya place the scrap of cloth carefully onto her other palm. The haunted house had never seemed like such a spine-chilling place. Her low voice chanted on:

"One-ery, two-ery, ickery, an,
Hokkani baro, just began.
Hakkni panki, so we see,
Toad, now put your luck on me."

Marya blew out the candles and all the magic disappeared as she said in her regular voice, "Now for the reading." She swished across the room to

where the cushions were piled. She pulled her old Heidi book out from the bottom of the stack and carried it back to where I stood feeling very ordinary in my plain jeans and T-shirt. She hesitated, then handed the book to me the same way our librarian hands you a book, as if she hates to part with it. Or just dares you to do anything damaging to it such as dropping it in a puddle or dog-earing a page.

The bookmark Walter had made for Marya stuck out showing how far he had already read to her. I glanced uneasily toward the doorway, remembering Marya's father, the *Rom Baro,* who hated *gorgios.* I wondered what was in the Heidi book that her father would be so angry about.

"What's the matter now?" Marya asked me.

"Your father doesn't ever come here, does he?" I asked, hating myself for letting her know I was scared.

She smiled as if that pleased her. "Don't fret," she said. "My father is a big man with moustaches clear to the ground, but he is a fair man. That is why he's the *Rom Baro.*"

I took a deep breath and opened the book to Walter's marker.

"Go ahead," Marya said in an impatient voice. "Start where Dete, the wicked aunt, has already left Heidi alone with the alm-uncle."

We sat down in the doorway and I began to read. But I stumbled over the word *astonishment* in about the fifth line. Marya muttered, "For sure you don't read as good as your little brother." I pretended I hadn't heard her and went on reading.

The book was pretty good. I read for about a half hour before I closed it and said I had to go home. I wanted to be sure and be there when Walter got back.

Marya took her book back, looking at me as if I *had* dog-eared a page.

"You *will* go to see Aunt Lolly first thing tomorrow, won't you?" I said as I stood up. "Her house is on Main Street, just a block past the courthouse." Then I described the house — how it was the tallest one, with fancy trimming, and the spiky fence around the tower room. "It's so different from the others, you'll know it easily," I promised. "You *can* speak Romany, can't you?"

Marya rattled off, "*Avah, mendui rakker sarja adovo jib. Boro kushto covva se ta rakker a jib te kek gorgio ünella.*"

"Hey, that's perfect," I said because the words really did sound beautiful the way she said them. "What does it mean?"

A teasing sort of a smile dented the tattoo on Marya's cheek. "It means, 'Yes, we always talk that language. It's nice to talk a language that no *gorgio* knows.' "

I have always wished I knew how to speak a secret language, too, so I sort of knew how she felt even if it wasn't very nice of her to say that in her language. "Do you think you could find Aunt Lolly's ring?" I asked.

Marya's dark eyes sparkled. "Sure I could," she said. "I could easy. Don't forget I'm a seventh daughter of a seventh daughter."

She acted so positive she could find that ring that I couldn't resist asking, "How? How can you, when you don't even know where she lost it?"

In that secretive way she had, Marya said, "A fox knows many things, but a Gypsy girl, more. The clue to where her ring is, is unconsciously in her own mind. No man knows how much he knows. When I look keenly into her eyes, with the vision given only to Gypsies, and look closely into her palm and tell her what I see there, then listen as only the Gypsies listen, she will say more than she knows. For me it is easy."

"Oh," I said, feeling awfully inferior with my plain old *gorgio* vision.

As I started down the rickety steps, Marya said, "Give your brother this message from me: '*Dell-o-del*.' "

I looked back suspiciously. "What does that mean?" I asked, not wanting to take any chances on delivering a Gypsy message that might make Walter worse.

"He will know," Marya said secretively.

I really did hate her!

Chapter
12

ALL THE WAY home my anger at Marya and my worry about Walter buzzed around my head like a cloud of creek mosquitoes.

My mother and Walter still weren't back. It was taking them awfully long. I wandered around the house a while and finally went out and sat on the front steps to watch for our car. When it turned into the driveway at last I got another shock. My mother was alone!

I ran to open the car door for her. "Where's Walter?" I cried.

My mother shook her head. "He had to stay over at the hospital for more tests," she said in a tired voice as she stepped out.

"Hospital! How long?" I asked trying to keep up with her, all the time assuring myself nervously that things would get better once Aunt Lolly talked to Marya.

"Not long. Katy, I have to call your father now," she said and went inside.

I hung around the kitchen to listen while my mother made the call. After she explained to my father about the tests, she said, "He's even having a little trouble breathing," and I heard her voice catch on an edge of fright.

So doctors didn't recognize spells. I *thought* a word to call Marya which my mother would never have allowed me to say. I knew what I was going to do, too!

I was going straight over to Aunt Lolly's house the minute I thought Marya would be there tomorrow morning. I wouldn't wait for Aunt Lolly to talk nicely to Marya. I would warn Marya that *she* was going to jail the same as her mother if she didn't take her spell off my brother — and fast. I'll scare her so bad she'll do what I say, I thought furiously. But I really knew from dealing with Marya that she wasn't easy to scare.

I sat at the kitchen table and watched as my mother got things out to start supper. Then she put them back and got them back out again. I felt like I was sitting alone in the bottom of a well.

It was a little better after my father came home. He's as matter-of-fact as Walter. I could hardly think about Walter without the end of my nose tingling miserably. Walter, alone in that hospital in the city and not even able to read.

While I dried the supper dishes I considered telling my mother about Marya and the spell. But I knew it would only make her worry worse than ever. She believed the doctor could cure allergies, but would she believe a Gypsy could take a spell back off him?

Chapter
13

THE NEXT MORNING when my mother left for the hospital I hurried to Aunt Lolly's big house. Every step of the way I thought about all the things Marya had done to Walter and me. When I got to the back door and heard Aunt Lolly's and Marya's voices inside, I even forgot to knock. I just threw open the heavy door and burst into the kitchen with the threatening words on the tip of my tongue.

But I stopped short in the middle of the room. Marya and Aunt Lolly were sitting at the kitchen table all right — just as I had expected them to be. But Marya was crying! Aunt Lolly was clucking and patting her shoulder.

I choked back the threatening words and instead said, "What's the matter with her?"

"Well you know, Dearie, her mother is in jail! She misses her, of course," Aunt Lolly said. Then she turned to Marya. "There, there, Dearie, she'll be out soon. All your people are helping. Now you can help, too."

Marya looked unexpectedly little and scared sitting there. I would hardly have known she was the same person who stole our haunted house, our toad, and put a spell on my brother. And she sure didn't seem like the same mystic person who had chanted the words about the Evil Eye.

The minute she saw me, Marya started wiping away her tears on her sleeve. *"Carranza,"* she said, only this time she said it in a weak, shaky little voice. "Do you have to bust in on me all the time?"

"Now, now," Aunt Lolly soothed, pulling a fancy handkerchief out of her dress and handing it to Marya. Then she looked at me. "Sit down, Katy, and let us tell you about our plan."

I eyed Marya warily, but pulled out one of the high-backed chairs and slid into it. Even now as she eyed me back suspiciously from across the table, Marya didn't seem like the same girl. She seemed plainer — smaller, here in Aunt Lolly's big, cozy kitchen. As if she didn't have to be so bossy and defensive, as if she just belonged — sort of naturally. If Aunt Lolly could change Marya so much this fast, surely she could get her to take her spell off fast, too. But then I thought of Walter, still in that hospital. I just couldn't take a chance. I leaned across the table toward Marya and blurted out, "You take your spell off my brother!"

Marya's dark eyes widened as if she was surprised to hear her spell was working so fast. I was scared that with such a successful spell going, she was going to say she'd never take it off. Instead she and Aunt Lolly looked at each other, and it seemed to me they already had a secret between them.

I stood up so fast my chair crashed to the floor. "If you don't, I'll have you put in jail just like your mother!" I yelled.

"Katy!" Aunt Lolly cried. "Be ashamed!"

Aunt Lolly had never talked to me in that voice before — like she was talking to a child. I felt bitter tears sting my eyes and knew more tears would follow.

I didn't wait to hear any more. It was plain to me that Aunt Lolly and Marya — one being a Gypsy and the other a True Rye — had already become better friends than Aunt Lolly and I were after all these years. I bolted for the back door, slamming it hard behind me.

Once I was outside I realized I had ruined Aunt Lolly's chances for helping me. I slowed down, hoping maybe Aunt Lolly might call me back. If she did I would apologize. But she didn't. Instead of being mad I was back to feeling scared again, and lonely, and, I guess, sorry for myself.

When I got home my mother still wasn't there.

I saw High-Pockets over in his backyard. I called to him and said I'd throw a few balls. It would help pass the time while I waited for news of Walter — or maybe even Walter himself. But the way things had gone at Aunt Lolly's I doubted that. If Walter isn't with Mother, I told myself, I'll tell my parents the whole story.

"I'll have to quit when my mother drives in," I said to High-Pockets. He knew, of course, about Walter being in the hospital. But even so I was surprised when he said, "You can quit whenever you want to, Katy."

I missed a couple of easy catches because I kept one eye out for our car. High-Pockets didn't say a word. At last I saw our blue station wagon turn into the driveway. Walter was in it!

I threw my glove down and took off for our yard. I opened the door on Walter's side. He looked pale, and thinner than he had just yesterday. But he hopped out without saying a word, just like his old self. Could spells come off that fast? "Is he all right?" I asked my mother.

She nodded happily. "He just has to rest a couple of days and go back for another allergy shot next week."

"Allergy?" I repeated dumbly. "Is that what the doctor thinks is wrong with him?"

"No, he isn't sure, Katy," mother said, following after Walter who was heading for the front door. "But whatever he had, it responded quickly this morning to a shot the doctor gave him. He thinks it might be the daisy fleabane blooming in the pasture. So of course Walter has to stay away until it stops blooming."

Was it the shot, or had Aunt Lolly convinced Marya to take away her spell? I thought of Marya's words: "The fox knows many things, but a Gypsy girl knows more." It was hard not to believe she had strange powers. And she *was* the seventh daughter of a seventh daughter. Aunt Lolly had said that meant she did have powers ordinary people — even ones ordinary Gypsies didn't have.

Inside my mother headed for the kitchen phone to let my father know Walter was home. I caught up with Walter as he started upstairs. "Was it awful?" I asked.

"Nope," he said exactly like his old self. "Did you get Babe Ruth back?"

I glanced toward the kitchen. "Not yet," I said in a low voice. "But I said I'd read to Marya until you came back, so I think she'll bring him soon." I didn't tell Walter about my deal with Marya. Now that Walter was better I was awfully ashamed of the way I'd acted at Aunt Lolly's that morning.

"Good," he said and went on up to his room.

For a long time I wandered around the house worrying about what had happened at Aunt Lolly's. We ate lunch, then my mother took Walter's food up to his room. When she came back she reported that he was reading again.

While I cleared the dishes I kept thinking about Marya crying because she missed her mother. I decided to go over to the haunted house and see if she showed up there. If she did, I'd say I was sorry and offer to read to her like I'd promised.

I wouldn't take any chances of crossing her again — no matter how mad she made me. After all, Walter was already better. And my mother believed it was because of the shot, and I hoped it was. But I couldn't be sure.

Chapter
14

WE HAD BEEN late eating lunch, and it was past two o'clock when I cut across Mr. Mortz's pasture. About halfway across I heard the faint sound of singing. I stopped to listen. It was coming from the haunted house. It must be Marya! It was sad, sweet singing that sounded like a violin playing. The notes seemed to be blown to me on the breeze that came from the direction of the woods.

I hurried toward the haunted house and the song got louder. It *was* Marya. I stopped on the bottom step and looked into the kitchen. Marya was dancing as she sang. Her bare feet were stamping, leaping, whirling; her red skirt swirling around her brown ankles. The golden loops in her ears flashed against her braids. The silver bracelets jingled, keeping time to the sweet, sad song.

> "I've seen you where,
> You never were,
> And where you never will be;
> And yet within that very place,
> You can be seen by me.
> For to tell what they do not know,
> Is the art of the Romany."

It was a throbbing, almost sobbing song. I stood there, spellbound. For the moment my old anger at her had melted away. With it gone I felt empty . . . lost. Marya made me feel so dull in my khaki shorts and faded blue T-shirt with my short, straight brown hair.

No wonder Marya didn't like me — or other *gorgios* either. *Gorgios* were ordinary, colorless people like daisy fleabane. Gypsies were like bright red poppies.

I tried to picture Marya's father, a giant man with moustaches reaching the ground — which I knew had to be an exaggeration — and her mother, a queen even if she was in jail.

Suddenly Marya seemed to sense I was standing there on the step. Her singing stopped. She whirled to face me.

I tightened up, expecting her to fly at me in a rage for spying again. Instead she said, "How is your brother Walter?"

I was so surprised, I told her the truth. "He's better."

She touched the tiny cloth drawstring bag she was wearing around her neck and smiled, denting in the little blue tattoo. "Did you give him my message: *Dell-o-del?*" she asked.

"No," I admitted, "because I didn't know what it meant. I was afraid it was part of the spell." I couldn't believe we were talking this way — without being enemies. It must be because of the white amulet, I thought.

"*Dell-o-del* only means 'God give you luck'," she said. Then she said something that made me know she was really not all that different from me. Something that made me think Aunt Lolly really had been on my side after all. She said, "Aunt Lolly told me you felt bad because you didn't pass fourth grade at your school. I know how you feel. It's like that for me when the other girls make fun of me because I can't read. Then I feel bad, too."

My head was whirling, things had changed so fast. We both stood there in an embarrassing little silence, then Marya said, "Come along, I have something to show you." She whirled around and headed for the narrow stair steps inside the front door.

I followed her up the steps, bypassing the missing second one and squeaking the third one in the usual way. I smelled the familiar dry, hot smell of the empty upstairs and felt sad remembering the many times we'd put Babe Ruth back in his cardboard home. I almost dared hope. . . .

And I was right. The little house had been set up straight again and there was Babe Ruth, fat and wise-looking as ever, sitting on the square of card-board cut out from where we'd made his front door.

I ran over and picked him up. He sat with his cool flat bottom side on my palm and stared at me in a very understanding way. I turned to Marya. "Gee, thanks!" I said, almost bawling for joy.

"That's sure one lucky toad," Marya said. "I figure without him I would never have met Aunt Lolly. I need that money to help get my mother free again."

I pictured her crying at Aunt Lolly's table. I thought how awful it would be after all, to have your very own mother eating her meals with the sheriff's family instead of your own. Even your mother being a queen wouldn't make up for that. I tried to think of something nice to say, but couldn't.

Babe Ruth still hadn't budged. I could tell he was as glad to see me as I was to see him by the way he kept hopping up and down on my palm, but not hopping off the way an ordinary toad would.

Finally I said, "Did you like Aunt Lolly?" As I said it my face skin tingled. I felt awful about the way I'd acted over there earlier.

"She's a True Rye for sure," Marya said. "She's almost as good as a Gypsy."

"Are you going back?" I asked, hoping she'd say yes.

Marya whirled her skirt, swaying a little as if she suddenly heard music I couldn't hear. Then she sort of sang, "Yes. Yes. For gold as you see, draws gold my dearie! She's going to pay me even more than this." She pulled out two one-dollar bills that I hadn't noticed tucked in the elastic ruffle of her sleeve. She waved them above her head.

"Did you find her ring already?" I asked, astonished at how much money she had.

"Not yet," Marya said. "This is for helping her out with her Romany. But I will find it because she's terrible fond of *dukkerin* and believes in it. She was surprised I knew of the missing ring. I might have said the spirits informed me of it in a dream. But I wanted things to be *caco* between us, so I told her you told me."

I decided *caco* must mean sort of like honest. I

was learning a secret language already. I tried to figure out what Aunt Lolly had done that had changed Marya so much.

"Do you want me to read to you now?" I asked.

"No, wait," Marya said as she folded the two bills. "Hey, see," she cried, "come along. You can watch me bury my money for safekeeping until my people and I have enough."

Marya led the way and I followed her down the stairs carrying Babe Ruth. I couldn't help thinking about the last time when I'd dashed down these stairs, angry and scared that Marya was going to set the old house on fire. It seemed like a long time ago.

When we were back in the kitchen again, Marya picked up her glass jar and carefully placed the folded money inside. She went down the steps to the back of the house so I sat on the bottom step to watch.

She stood with her shoulders pressed against the outside wall of the house, facing the woods. Then she stepped off seven long steps. She counted each one out loud. After the seventh, she put her jar on the ground, got down on her knees and began to pull up clumps of the tough pasture grass. When she had a big enough bare spot, she asked me to go get the stick from her three-legged kettle.

When I brought it from inside, she stood over the bare spot with the stick between her palms and began whirling the pointed end of the three-pronged stick round and round into the soft, damp dirt. As the stick dug into the ground she chanted,

> "Straw, draw, crow caw.
> By my life I give thee law.
> Spirit of earth, spirit of sky,
> Let this treasure safely lie."

When the dirt was loosened deep enough to suit her, she got down and scooped the hole clean with her hands. She laid the jar with the money in it carefully into the hole. Then she filled the hole and hid the spot with the clumps of grass.

From my palm Babe Ruth watched as closely as I did while Marya stood up and lifted the drawstring bag from around her neck. She took out a pinch of the Evil Eye powder. As she sprinkled the powder over the spot she said, "Garlic, garlic, garlic." Then she turned to me and whispered. "That will keep the Evil Eyed person from discovering where the money was buried."

I wanted to ask how, but I only nodded.

"That's done," she said, whisking her hands together. "Now we can read." She went past me sitting there on the step and came right back and handed me her Heidi book.

"You watch Babe Ruth," I said and put him in the beat-down grass around the bottom step. I opened the book to Walter's leather marker and began reading. This time I didn't stumble over hardly any words — only a few long ones. When I did, Marya didn't say anything about my reading. Things sure were different between us.

That book really wasn't so bad. In fact it was pretty interesting. The mountain grandfather was halfway between being mysteriously scary and being kind. Even the cheese and goat's milk, which I'm sure I'd hate, sounded very good in the story.

Time went by real fast and finally I could tell by the sun I'd better get home.

Marya went upstairs with me to put Babe Ruth in his house. She followed along without saying a word. I supposed she was thinking about the story, which was on my mind, too. It was hard to come back to the haunted house after feeling as if you were up on that mountain top.

When we were downstairs again and I said good-bye, Marya answered, "*Dell-o-del.*" She grinned at me in a friendly way for worrying about what that meant earlier.

I smiled back thinking that this was exactly like a secret time between friends. As I hurried across Mr. Mortz's pasture I felt better about things than I had all summer. And yet there was a strange little warning ticking inside my head, telling me to beware of this happiness. Like a Gypsy prophecy, I thought.

Chapter
15

FOR ALMOST A week things went along so smoothly between Marya and me that it made the bad that followed seem even worse.

Walter got much better, but still had to stay indoors. I went to read to Marya every afternoon. The book got more and more exciting. When my mother asked me what I did over there without Walter, I could honestly tell her I liked to go there to read.

Before we read each day, Marya dug up her jar and added the money she'd earned in the morning from Aunt Lolly. I knew the little chant by heart by then because she said it each time.

"Straw, draw, crow caw.
By my life I give thee law.
Spirit of earth, spirit of sky,
Let this treasure safely lie."

I learned lots of other Gypsy things, too. And more Gypsy words, like *diklo,* which meant the silk scarf Marya wore around her dark curly hair when it wasn't in braids. I'd purposely fit these words into my conversations with Marya. Words like *caco, Hokanni baro, gorgio,* and *Dell-o-del.*

Oh, there was also *carranza,* which Marya used to say when she was mad at me. I suspected from the tone of her voice when she said it that it was one of those words our mother won't let us even think.

The troubled times really began because of the Evil Eye. Whenever Marya said that word she lowered her voice so that it sounded terribly dark and fearful. "If a person with the Evil Eye looks upon you," she told me, "you become bewitched and many troubles will befall you."

Marya worried a lot about being looked upon by the Evil Eye. There was that brew she made in her kettle the first time we saw her when she was saying the scary chant. Some of the powder from it was still there. The skull on the post was to keep the Evil Eye away, too. Even the tiny tattoo on Marya's cheek had been put there when she was a baby to protect her from the Evil Eye. And the egg in the doorway was there to stop anyone with the Evil Eye from entering our haunted house.

But as it turned out, none of these things Marya believed in worked. I guess Marya sensed that the

Evil Eye was lurking nearby one day when, after we'd finished reading, I asked her to tell my fortune.

When I asked, she looked doubtful. "I don't think so," she said.

"Please, Marya," I begged. "I've never had my fortune told."

But Marya shook her head. "I can't do *dukkerin* for you, Katy. I know you too deep. Anyway, what do I know? I'm just a Gypsy."

"You're a seventh daughter," I said. "That's even better than being a Gypsy. And besides, you're my best friend."

"And you're a True Rye, Katy," Marya said. "You and Aunt Lolly both are. But Katy, you're so funny. You've got to understand — me saying I'm only a Gypsy is just the way we Gypsies talk when we're talking to *gorgios*. You know what I'm saying?"

"No," I said stubbornly. "And I think you just don't want to tell my fortune."

"But I'd like your understanding," Marya pleaded. "Me saying I'm just a Gypsy is like us Gypsies saying we never have any luck when we know we're the luckiest ones — never having to be *of* the world, but always living by woods and streams. Knowing the sweetness of nature. And hearing voices in the wind."

"You're trying to change the subject," I accused. "Aunt Lolly's Gypsy friend, Volga, told *her* fortune.

Is it because I don't have any money?"

Marya's eyes flashed sparks. " 'Course not!" Then she shrugged. "So as you wish to hear it, then I will." But she looked across each of her shoulders as if she felt some other presence there in the haunted house.

She brought us both one of her pillows and we sat down on the floor.

For what seemed like a long time Marya just sat there with her head bent, looking at the palm of my hand. I began to get a creepy feeling along the tops of my shoulders. Was she seeing a picture at the base of my thumb the way she had once said she could — *if* the person believed. I tried hard to believe Marya could really see my future there.

When she finally started talking her voice was hushed and seemed almost to be coming out of the stillness in the crumbling walls instead of from her. "I see you're a good person," she said. "You're honest and you smile in your face. But wait, now I see that you no longer smile the way you should. I see you tossing and turning in your bed. Something's troubling you now for sure."

I listened, hypnotized as I always was when Marya talked that way. She let go of my hand, lifted her drawstring bag from her neck, and took out a pinch of her Evil Eye powder. She took my hand again and sprinkled the palm with powder. A little shiver went over me as she blew the powder away. "Listen to me," she said. "Quickly make two wishes. Keep one to yourself and tell me the other."

"I wish you'd find Aunt Lolly's diamond ring," I said in a whisper.

Marya looked into my palm again and nodded.

"Okay I've got the second one," I said. "It's about you and me."

Marya looked into my eyes, then back down at my palm. She shook her head. "It won't come true," she said sadly. When she looked back up at me again there were tears in her eyes.

I didn't know what to say. I just sat there dumb as wood, wishing I'd never asked her to do this in the first place. I'd never dreamed it would be like this. I thought she'd talk about a trip and a tall handsome man in my future.

Marya swallowed hard and said, "You have not chosen your secret wish wisely. The spirits are displeased with you." Suddenly she pushed my hand away. "I told you I knew you too deep, Katy." She pulled off her *diklo* and wiped her eyes with it.

I touched her arm. "But you don't even know what my secret wish was," I said.

Marya jumped up from the floor. "I know more than I want to know," she said, sounding almost angry. Then she said she had to go home. I knew that no matter what it was that had upset her, it wasn't anything she blamed me for. But as I watched her hurry off toward the woods carrying her bag with the three X's, I felt unbearably sad. *"Dell-o-del,"* I whispered after her.

Chapter
16

THE NEXT DAY, hours before anything happened, I felt restless. All morning I hid out from High-Pockets because I didn't feel like playing catch. I kept wishing the time would come to go meet Marya.

Walter was well and sort of wandering around, too. After lunch he went with me when I cut across the pasture to the haunted house.

Marya said she was glad to see Walter, but she looked like she'd never be really glad about anything again. Walter went right upstairs and brought Babe Ruth down. Walter didn't seem to sense yet that anything was wrong. I hadn't told him about my fortune. I hadn't felt like discussing it with anyone.

When I read Marya's Heidi book even Walter said I did a good job. But I didn't read long because Marya didn't seem to have her mind on the story. I wondered if she was thinking about the things she'd read in my palm the day before. Maybe she hadn't told me everything. Maybe I was *never* going to pass fourth grade!

After Marya hid the book back under the pillows she told us she was going to show us how to make Gypsy *patrins*. "You may have need of them some-day," she said darkly. As it turned out, she was right.

She explained that Gypsy *patrins* were little signs that the Gypsies leave for one another. They're made out of twigs, rocks, and thread.

One kind of *patrin* points out the path of Gypsies who have gone on ahead of the others. There are *patrins* that tell what's up, like, "business is good here" or "food for the picking nearby." The *patrin* Marya was making was to warn of trouble.

"If ever in your life you are in trouble and need help," Marya told Walter and me, "leave one of these where a Gypsy will find it. Gypsies never fail to help someone in trouble — even a *gorgio*," she added with a little shadow of a smile.

Walter looked at me sort of puzzled as if he'd like me to give him a clue to why Marya was acting this way. But I only shrugged and he and I watched in silence as Marya twisted thread around two sticks so they looked like a cross.

Suddenly she began to sing in such a small voice that I could barely catch the words:

By a spell to me unknown,
I never more shall be alone.
When the frost is on the tree,
A million words will comfort me.
Intery, mintery, cutery corn,
Ingle 'em, angle 'em, every dawn."

Then she blew out the candle. But just as the flame flickered and went out I heard a little plop from the doorway. Startled, I turned to look. The egg, which had hung by the thread all this time, had dropped to the floor. It had smashed to pieces. For a split second none of us moved.

There was a terrible smell. Walter pinched his nose together and looked at Marya. She got up slowly and went over and picked up the biggest piece of shell. Then she dropped it as if it had been hot and cried out, "*Carranza!* The yoke — " She covered her eyes with her hands.

I hurried to her and put my arm around her shoulder. She was shaking.

"Oh Katy," she whispered, "I had no business wanting to know what was in books. The Evil Eye has looked upon me now. A curse is on this house! I could sense it ever since I told that fortune for you."

I looked down at the broken egg. In the piece of shell Marya had dropped there was a tiny red

blob in the egg yoke, but otherwise it just looked like a rotten egg to me. "Maybe it's only a little curse," I said. I wished I could do something to keep her from being so frightened.

Marya shook her head. "We got to get out of here."

"But your book, your things — " I began looking around the room frantically.

Walter interrupted in his calm voice. "I'll put Babe Ruth back upstairs." He reached toward our toad which still hadn't moved.

"No!" Marya said. "We're not going upstairs, and we're not leaving him here alone either. I'll take him home with me for the night. And my book, too." She picked up her book and slipped it into her bag. Then she picked up Babe Ruth and put him carefully in beside it. She closed her eyes and chanted in a scared voice:

"Toad in my bag,
Devour what is bad.
Toad in my bag,
Show the evil the way out."

Without a word to us she turned and hurried out the back doorway. Walter and I followed her, stepping with care around the fallen egg.

When we were outside I said, "We *will* meet here tomorrow, won't we?" I glanced back inside the haunted house. "Surely there's some way you can get rid of the curse."

"I'll bring more things and try," Marya said as she headed toward the woods. Walter and I watched her until she was lost in the trees.

Chapter 17

THAT NIGHT I dreamed the Evil Eye spread a heavy, black blanket over the whole haunted house with Walter, Marya, and me trapped inside. While I was still only half awake I tried to recall from my dream what the Evil Eye had looked like, but couldn't.

My next thought, fully awake now, was of Marya. Had the Evil Eye really looked upon her? Had she gone to Aunt Lolly's this morning as usual? Maybe Aunt Lolly, who knew all about spirits and charms, could tell her what to do about the curse on the haunted house.

Later, when the dark, cloudy morning had finally turned into afternoon, Walter and I hurried over to the haunted house not knowing what to expect.

The minute we reached the back steps I saw I'd been right to worry. Stuck in the ground was a message — two sticks tied with thread. Marya's trouble *patrin!*

From the top step we peeked cautiously into the kitchen. The inside was silent and dark as if a black blanket had really been thrown over the house, smothering out all the sound and light. Marya wasn't in the kitchen.

Staying close together Walter and I crept on inside the doorway. The egg had dried to a sticky, smelly mess with little pieces of shell caught in it. We called out Marya's name, but it was no use. The house was empty.

We moved on through the rest of the house as slowly as if we'd never been in it before and didn't know our way — or what was ahead for us! I knew Walter was thinking the same as I was — that we *had* to go upstairs. We had to see if Babe Ruth was back in his house.

The creaky stair step seemed creakier and the stairway even darker and narrower, trapping the rotten egg smell between the musty walls. Still, we had to know.

Babe Ruth wasn't there. Marya had not brought him when she came to leave us the trouble *patrin* message. I had a sudden, awful thought. Maybe some other Gypsy had left the trouble *patrin*. Maybe the *Rom Baro* had! Maybe he had left it as a warning for us to stay away from Marya.

I scolded myself that I must have caught my mother's worry habit. But I nudged Walter and whispered, "Let's get out of here."

Once we were outside again I said, hoping Walter would agree, "We have to go to the Gypsy camp."

Every year our church has its picnic in Walnut Grove, so we'd been there lots of times. Walter nodded.

About a quarter of a mile before we reached the grove I heard a faint, far-off sound. I put out my hand to stop Walter. "Listen," I said.

"Music," Walter said and we started racing up the gravel road. If that was Gypsy music then at least the camp was still there!

Sure enough, the farther we went the louder the music was. Who but Gypsies would be making music on a cloudy morning in the country?

The music told us we were getting closer. The sound of it was almost like a natural part of the outdoors. Music like the wind makes in trees, along with the sound of water over rocks, and maybe some crickets and birds chiming in. But this was real music all right — music played with some sort of instruments.

When we were almost to the narrow wooden bridge where Prairie Dog Creek crosses the road I slowed down and said to Walter, "Marya told me it was bad luck to cross a bridge without first spitting three times over the rail."

There wasn't any rail to this little bridge, but Walter and I quickly spit into the water three times anyway. We needed all the luck we could get. Luck that we'd find Marya, that she'd be okay. And luck that her father wouldn't see us.

We hurried on up the road again, following the sad-happy music. We could tell for sure now it was coming from Walnut Grove just ahead. As we ran along I vowed to myself that no matter what kind of trouble Marya was in, Walter and I would help her.

When we reached the edge of the grove I stopped and said real quietly, "I think we'd better cut through so we can stay hidden behind trees. And for Pete's sake, Walter, if you need to sneeze, do it now."

"I don't," Walter assured me. We cut over to the side of the road, down the ditch and up the bank. There isn't any fence around Walnut Grove and the trees are close together.

Before we even were halfway through the woods the music stopped. Now we could hear people talking and laughing. A dog barked. I hoped it wouldn't hear or smell us coming. But I decided if we were going to contact Marya we'd have to take our chances.

As the voices got plainer we got more careful dodging from one tree to the next. I was looking down, watching where I stepped so I wouldn't pop a dry branch when I saw it! I stopped dead still and stared, too shocked to pick it up. It was Marya's Heidi book!.

Chapter
18
___

WALTER SAW THE book, too. He looked slowly around as if to make sure no one was watching before he bent down and picked it up.

The front cover was bent back and almost broken. The back cover was gone. The pages were all swollen from dampness. Walter brushed the dirt away with his long-sleeved shirt and handed the book to me.

Discovering Marya's precious book almost ruined gave me the creepy feeling something terrible *had* happened to Marya herself. I knew how important that book was to her. I knew she had to keep it hidden, but I was positive she would never hide it out here in the woods.

It was a horrible thought, but I couldn't believe that Marya, alive, would let this happen to the one possession she loved more than anything else in the world.

When Walter and I were almost to the far edge of the woods we came up a little rise, and there was the Gypsy camp spread out in O'Riley's meadow. Only the creek separated us from it.

Walter and I ducked behind the same big tree. The lower end of the meadow was filled with low, round tents. Brightly painted Gypsy wagons and trailers stood beside them. The Gypsies themselves — at least a lot of them — were sitting in a big circle on the ground. There were men, women, and children dressed in every gay color there is. They were laughing and shouting back and forth to one another.

The tent nearest the circle of people was decorated with flowers and leaves. My heart pounded as I searched the circle, hoping to see Marya.

And there she was, wedged in between two fat Gypsy women. She was scrunched down and her face wasn't happy and smiling like everyone else's.

A couple of skinny dogs were wandering around. There was a big square of canvas stretched over four poles to make a sort of roof. This must be the *dingle*. Campfires were burning beneath the canvas cover. There was a table covered with a white cloth. But the only people over near the table were some little kids laughing and chasing each other.

Walter and I ducked back as two old Gypsy men got up from the circle and headed toward the *dingle*. When I thought it was safe I peeked out again. The men had silk *diklos* around their curly gray hair. One was smoking a fancy pipe. The other wore a gold loop like Marya's, but only in one ear.

I looked back at Marya. How were we going to let her know we had come? I knew we had to stay hidden because Marya had made it plain that her father didn't like *gorgios* one bit.

While I was still trying frantically to think of some way to signal Marya, the music started up again. The musicians were standing in the center of the circle of people. One was playing a violin, one a tambourine, and the other an accordion. We were so close to the music now, that it seemed to melt right into my bones and make them ache.

All at once a man came striding down to the circle from one of the tents. I grabbed Walter's arm. I was sure he must be Marya's father, the *Rom Baro!* Of course he didn't actually have "moustaches reaching the ground" the way Marya had told us. But the ends of his moustache came way below his chin. He was extra tall and fat, too, with a big head and long arms — just the way Marya had described him.

He was wearing a red sash and gold loops in both ears. He had on a vest with golden buttons and a necklace made of gold coins. I shivered and hugged Marya's book tighter when I saw the jeweled hilt of a knife gleaming from his waistband. He had to be the *Rom Baro.*

Then I gasped so loud Walter punched me to remind me we were hiding. Without any warning the music changed to the wedding march and out of another tent came a tall girl followed by a shorter girl.

I stared at the taller girl. She was wearing a long white gown. She was as beautiful as Marya and not much older. I was almost sure she was Marya's sister.

She had a crown of jewels on her head. They absolutely sparkled. Hanging from her crown were red, blue, and yellow ribbons that fell over each side of her face.

I wondered which of the Gypsy boys she was marrying. All the boys in the circle were handsome, with curly black hair and flashing smiles. I wondered if Marya would have a wedding like this some day. I looked at her again. From the look on her face I knew she wasn't enjoying this celebration. What *was* she thinking about right now? Why had her book been lying in the woods? Why had she left us the trouble *patrin*?

The bride was singing a sad song. Something about having to leave her own mother and go to live with her husband's family. I looked at Marya again. I was sure she was crying. Was Marya thinking about *her* own mother, Queen Millie Rose who was in jail?

Suddenly the music turned joyful and wild. The bride swooped up a long, filmy red scarf from the ground and began to dance. As she danced she floated the scarf across the face of one of the Gypsy boys in the circle as if she was choosing him from the others.

The boy leaped to his feet and caught the other end of the scarf. They danced together then, laughing and flirting with each other.

The people in the circle began to clap in time to the music. It seemed as if the tempo of the music changed how the people felt.

All the people except Marya. As I watched her again, she looked in the direction of the woods. Had she sensed we were hiding there? Or was she thinking of her book? Then she turned sadly back toward the bride and groom.

The music and dancing stopped. I hugged the tree trunk with my one free hand as I clasped the book with the other. The huge man with the long moustaches stepped inside the circle with the girl and boy. He said to the girl, "Go, Lenka, and fetch bread, salt, and water."

The bride called Lenka disappeared into the tent decorated with flowers. She came right back carrying a basket over one arm and a clay jug in the other.

The Rom Baro took a loaf of bread from the basket the girl held. He broke off two pieces. He sprinkled something on each piece. I couldn't see from there where he got the stuff to sprinkle with. Then he fed one bite to Lenka and one to the groom.

I watched as if I were under a spell as the *Rom Baro* lifted the jug and held it first for the bride, then the groom, to drink from. I jumped, startled, when, after they had drunk, the Rom Baro dashed the jug to the ground and stomped it to pieces.

Then his words thundered out, "As many pieces as there are here, will be the years of your happiness together. Keep one piece each. Preserve it carefully, and only if you lose it will misery and loneliness come upon you."

I looked at the spot where Marya had been sitting. She was gone!

There was a crackling sound in the woods behind us. I whirled around. At first I didn't see anything. Then back away, through a tangle of bushes I caught a glimpse of color, and Marya herself popped into sight.

She *must* have sensed we were here!

But she looked as surprised to see us as I was to see her. Making hardly a sound she ran toward the tree where we'd been hiding. "Katy! Walter!" she cried softly. "You came!" When she was almost beside us she saw the book I was clutching. She stopped short. "You found it!" she whispered. "You found my book!"

She reached for it so eagerly I knew for sure she hadn't hidden her book in the woods.

When I handed it to her she began smoothing the crinkled pages with tears in her eyes. "I couldn't resist getting it out to look at the pictures. By accident my father caught me with it," she said as if pleading with us to understand. "He was angry. He threw it into the woods. Until now, when everyone will be busy with the *abiv* — the wedding feast — I didn't dare take a chance looking for it."

She glanced toward the camp where now the Gypsies were all standing in noisy groups eating, and drinking from shiny goblets. "I'm scared," she said. "My father says the Evil Eye has looked on me for learning *gorgio* ways. I *have* learned much from the *gorgio* book already, and it frightens me. We can't read anymore. I will never know what happens to Heidi and Clara."

Panic tightened my throat, but I managed to whisper, "You *will* come back to the haunted house, though?"

"I don't know," Marya said with tears spilling out of her dark eyes. "My father — " She broke off. Then she swallowed hard and went on. "There are evil spirits in the house now — because of the book. I shouldn't have made *diwano* for learning to read." She looked down kicking with her sandal at the moss around the tree. Then she looked back at me

121

and smiled through her tears. "As you want me to so much, I will come," she said. I felt a little better.

Marya looked toward the camp again. "*He* knows when something's wrong. You better go. Next is the *zeita* — the real marriage ceremony. If they catch you watching that — *Please* go."

She looked so miserable that my heart felt like it was crumbling to bits for her. "Promise one thing," I begged. "*Promise* you'll come to the haunted house like you agreed."

Marya nodded. "Here then, put my book back under my pillows where it will be safe."

I took the book and whispered, "*Dell-o-del,*" and touched her shoulder. Then I quick turned away before she could see I was about to cry, too. "Come on, Walter," I called over my shoulder.

We ran back through Walnut Grove with the sad sound of Gypsy music beginning to race through the leaves above us.

Chapter
19

WHEN WE CAME out of the thick trees on the road side of Walnut Grove I noticed the clouds were heavier and darker. By the time we reached Prairie Dog Creek, the wind, which had been blowing in our faces, suddenly changed. Now it blew at our backs as if it were trying to push us toward home because our mother was worrying.

"Hurry, Walter," I urged him because all at once it seemed as if we'd been in some faraway land — and for a long time.

"Still have to hide Marya's book like we promised," Walter reminded me.

The sky was threatening rain any minute by the time we reached Mr. Mortz's pasture. But still I waited a second for Walter to catch up with me before I went on inside the haunted house.

I looked around uneasily. Marya's things were scattered all around. The leaves on the *diwano* box-table were faded and curling at the edges. The burned candles seemed like a bad omen.

Walter looked toward the tattered tapestry curtain sagging down on one side. "Seems awfully deserted around here," he said.

"Except for the Evil Eye," I said shuddering. I tiptoed quickly across to the pillows and stuck Marya's Heidi book between them. "Let's go," I whispered, starting for the back doorway.

That night after supper our whole family was together in the kitchen. While Mother washed dishes and Father dried them, I sat at the cleaned-off table thinking about Marya.

My brother Ben's girl friend was there. They were popping corn and talking about school next fall. I couldn't help thinking how different they were from Lenka the Gypsy bride and her groom.

Just then Walter, who was sitting across from me reading from one of my encyclopedia books, looked up. Walter was the only person in the room who could possibly understand how mixed-up I felt. I could tell by the way he looked at me that for once his mind was not on the book he had in front of him. It was the same place mine was — back at the Gypsy camp with Marya.

Some day, I thought, *I* will pack up my belongings and travel with a caravan to the sea marshes and live off the land — cook hot stews over a peat fire the way Marya had told me her people sometimes did.

I vowed that even though I *had* been born a *gorgio,* when I grew up I would live like those Gypsies were. I was grateful that at least Walter, who was back to wanting to do whatever I did, would probably be glad to go along with me. Yes, some day Walter and I would "raggle taggle after Gypsies" the way Aunt Lolly's mama had.

Chapter
20

SOME TIME LATER that night a big storm hit Tarryville. I woke up and saw my mother in her robe shutting my windows. The lightning was splitting the sky outside. "Go on back to sleep, Katy," my mother said. "It's just a rain storm." But I could tell by her voice she was nervous.

I couldn't get back to sleep. The wind began howling, and the thunder was so loud it rattled my windows. I couldn't help worrying about Marya in that camp with maybe only a tent around her. I tried to assure myself that probably the *Rom Baro* would live in one of the traveling wagons. But even those could have blown over in this fierce wind.

After a while the wind and rain both stopped and it got deathly quiet. I had just started to drift off to sleep again when somebody snapped on the hall light. I heard someone running in the hallway. I threw back my cover and dashed to my door in time to see our mother and father hurrying down the steps.

I ran after them to see what was wrong. Walter came down the stairs right behind me so I knew he'd heard the commotion, too.

When I got to the kitchen our parents were standing in the open back doorway. I could smell smoke even before I saw what was happening.

The haunted house was on fire!

I crowded in front of my parents and screamed, "*No! Stop it! Stop it!*" out into the night.

My mother put her arm around me. "It's all right, Katy," she said.

But it wasn't. That fire was a terrible thing to look at! Flames were shooting out the windows in front, and up through the roof. They lit up all that part of the pasture so we could see the great ugly rolls of black smoke pouring out. I started sobbing so hard I almost threw up.

My mother squeezed her arms tighter around my shoulder. "Now Katy," she said, "it's only an empty old house."

But it wasn't an empty old house. It was our haunted house! Marya's book was there — her *things*. But not Babe Ruth, I remembered thankfully. I tried to stop crying, but I couldn't. And I couldn't stop looking at that terrible sight either, even though it was the worst sight I had ever seen.

I looked at Walter and tears were streaming

down his face, too. I reached over and squeezed his hand. Lights went on at High-Pocket's house and the Rayhills on the other side. We could see neighbors out by the fence now, but it was too dark to see who they were — just their silhouettes.

Pretty soon we heard the sirens of the Tarryville fire truck. The truck pulled up into our driveway since that was as close to the haunted house as they could drive. The men from the volunteer fire department jumped down and ran toward the fire.

I heard our father say, "Lightning struck it, I'll bet." But I thought about the Evil Eye.

The whole house was in flames now. We could see the outlines of the firemen. They were beating the grass around the house where the fire had spread, even though the grass was wet from the rain. I knew there wasn't anything the firemen could do but let the haunted house burn clear down.

One of the shadowy figures from the fence came over to sit on our back steps. It was Mr. Rayhill. Father went out to join him. With a start I realized what Mr. Rayhill was saying. "It's a shame. Heard old man Mortz say he was planning to store hay in it this fall. Gypsies did it. No doubt about it. Getting even for us holding their queen in jail."

"No!" I thought I shouted, but no sound came from my throat. Beside me Walter made a sudden move forward so I knew he'd heard Mr. Rayhill, too. I threw out my arm to stop him. He'd only give away our secret.

But then I remembered Marya's three-legged kettle! It would never burn! Would they find it in the ashes and trace it to a Gypsy — to Marya? Would Marya get blamed for the fire if she came to meet us when she left Aunt Lolly's tomorrow?

I moved closer to Walter and whispered, "We *have* to warn her first thing in the morning!"

Chapter
21

MOTHER LET US watch until the house was clear gone. When the flames began to die it got pitch dark in the pasture. At last the firemen came back and drove their truck away. Our mother said we'd better all get to bed.

After I finally got to sleep I dreamed Marya and Walter and I were in the upstairs of the haunted house when it burned. I dreamed we had to jump out an upstairs window. In my dream High-Pockets caught each one of us as we jumped. Then he threw us to the firemen and they threw us onto their truck. Just as the fire truck drove away with us, I woke up and my heart was pounding. It was beginning to get light outside. I could tell the sun was going to shine.

The first thing I thought of was that Walter and I had to get to the Gypsy camp quick before Marya left for Aunt Lolly's.

I pulled on a pair of shorts and T-shirt and went to wake Walter. While he dressed I went downstairs and looked out the back door.

Even knowing the house would be gone didn't prepare me for that awful empty place where it had been. There was nothing left except some black boards stacked like jackstraws, with little smoke curls rising from the charred heap.

I was still standing, staring and trying not to start crying again when Walter came down. He stood there beside me a minute. Neither of us said a word. There wasn't anything to say.

Finally Walter turned back toward the kitchen. "Hurry, Katy," he said in a sad voice, "or everybody will be up. They'll make us eat breakfast."

"We'll leave a note," I said.

Walter got the pencil and pad from beside the telephone. I wrote, "Don't worry. Went for a hike."

Walter propped the note on the table and we started off. The sun was up now. The air outside smelled bitter from wet burned wood. From the fence we could see the cement post still standing. It was the only thing that hadn't changed. But then when we got closer we saw that the horse's skull was gone.

We stopped just a minute beside the smoldering boards which just yesterday were our haunted house. My nose began to itch like it does just before I start crying, so I said, "Better get going."

We didn't talk any more all the way through the

woods back of the pasture, not until we came to Prairie Dog bridge and had spit into the creek three times. Then as we hurried on up the road I said, "We'll have to tell her about her book, too."

"Let's run," Walter said. So we did.

We soon came to the edge of Walnut Grove, dashed across the ditch and hurried cautiously through the trees toward the Gypsy camp.

We didn't slow down until we came to the little rise in the ground at the far edge of the trees. Then we stopped dead still, too startled to speak. I clutched Walter's shoulder in dismay.

Walter muttered, "Gone!"

I just stood there. It seemed as if my whole world was disappearing. I'll never see Marya again, I thought, staring at the worn spots of earth in O'Riley's meadow through a film of tears.

I could tell which worn place was the square where the *dingle* had been. The smaller worn spots showed where the tents had been, and the pale yellowed grass where wagons had been parked. Gone. Everything was gone — as if the storm last night had swept it all away.

Walter sighed. "I guess she was right about the curse on the haunted house," he said.

I nodded, too choked to say anything.

"Better go home," Walter said. "Mother will

worry." He turned away and I followed him back through the trees. It seemed as if my heart was beating in my head instead of my chest. I could almost hear a faint echo of Gypsy music on the breeze scattering the first leaves of fall around us.

I'll never know anybody like Marya again, I thought, as we walked along the road. Things in my life will never be new and exciting again — the way they were when I had her for a friend.

As we crossed the bridge again, without even spitting this time, I felt goose bumps on my arms and shivered. Summer's over, I thought. Everything's over.

This time I passed the burned down haunted house without even looking at it. I stared straight ahead so I wouldn't have to see.

As we were climbing through the fence, Walter said, "She does have Babe Ruth to bring her luck with her *dukkerin*." Then he added, "Maybe she had time to get her book before they left. Before it burned."

"Maybe," I said. I pushed open our back door. "And her money!" I added in a whisper because our mother was in the kitchen. "We'll check right after we eat!"

"Right," Walter whispered back. "If her money's gone we'll know she got her book, too."

"What are you two whispering about so early in the morning?" our mother asked cheerfully. Without waiting for us to answer she said, "Come along and sit down. Your eggs and cinnamon toast are ready."

I could tell by her voice she was trying to make up to us for the haunted house burning. Even though she's the worrying kind of mother, she always knows what you feel sad or glad about.

To make her feel better I tried to say, "It really was just an empty old house," but I choked on the words. If there was anything the haunted house *wasn't,* it was empty!

I bit into my toast and the cinnamon tasted like dust. I knew I would never smell cinnamon again without thinking about Marya.

When Walter had finished eating I hurried to scrape the food off my plate into the garbage pail before my mother saw I hadn't eaten it. As we went out the back door our mother said, "Don't get too close to those burned boards. There'll be rusty nails."

The pile of black boards had almost stopped smoking now, but the damp smoke smell was still strong. With a heavy heart I counted off the seven steps from the foundation of the haunted house. The grass was scorched and it took us a minute to find the exact spot.

I pulled away the burnt grass and scooped out

the dirt. The fruit jar with the money in it was still there!

For a second neither of us touched it. We both just squatted there looking at it. The dollar bills inside the jar were crumpled so we couldn't tell how many there were, but it looked like quite a few.

"We should take the money back to Aunt Lolly," I said listlessly. Now that Marya was gone nothing seemed important.

Walter lifted the jar from the hollow space. He handed it to me. I took the bills out and straightened each one. There were fourteen of them. "Twice seven, a lucky number," I said bitterly.

"Let's bury the empty jar again," Walter said.

I agreed. It seemed like the right thing to do. After we had patted the last clump of grass into place I stuck the money into my pocket.

Back home, when we asked Mother if we could go visit Aunt Lolly, she said cheerily to be home in time for lunch because she was going to make dried beef gravy on toast. It wasn't even the day for it.

We knocked on Aunt Lolly's back door and she called, "Come in, Dearie." The next thing I noticed brought me to a stumbling stop. Sitting on the pink lace tablecloth, right in front of Aunt Lolly, was Babe Ruth!

"How — Where — " I stammered, too surprised to do anything but stand dumbly pointing at him.

"Marya left him here for you, Dearie," Aunt Lolly said, giving her tiara a little push.

"Where *is* she? When did she come? What's happened?" I cried.

"Sit down and have your tea, and I'll tell you all about it," Aunt Lolly said.

Walter had picked up Babe Ruth, and he was hopping up and down on Walter's hand like he was clowning to try to make me happy again.

I spilled tea all over, I was in such a hurry to find out more. Aunt Lolly didn't seem to notice the spilled tea. "The Gypsy caravan came through Tarryville on its way out of town," she began. "They stopped up the street there at the courthouse to pick up Marya's mama. Marya ran down here while they were taking care of the fine. She said the very first thing I must tell you, Katy, was this: A Gypsy never forgets a road he has traveled."

"Why — " I began, my hopes soaring because I thought maybe I already knew.

"It means she'll be back another summer, Dearie," Aunt Lolly said, giving my hand an understanding pat.

Another summer. *Next* summer! Suddenly everything seemed much better.

"When did they leave?" I asked, needing to know every detail.

"Late yesterday afternoon," Aunt Lolly said. "I was expecting it, you know. Foretold to me by the wind change. Few Gypsies can resist setting out on the change of the wind."

I took Marya's money out of my pocket and laid it on the table. "This is yours now," I said.

Aunt Lolly picked up the money and put it back in my hands. "Keep it for her," she said. "She told me she didn't mind leaving it behind because her people had gathered enough to pay Queen Millie's fine." I knew now what I was going to do with the money.

I knew what I was going to do about Marya's

Heidi book, too. When next summer came I would go to the library and check out that book. Marya and I would finish the story together. Until then I wouldn't even peek inside the book. "The haunted house — pasture house — burned down last night," I told Aunt Lolly.

"I heard," Aunt Lolly said. "Mrs. McJimsy, who was helping me out earlier this morning, told me."

"And Marya told me she was about to find your ring," I said. I didn't want her to lose faith in Marya's *dukkerin*.

"Oh, my ring." Aunt Lolly tilted her head and her face turned pink. "Oh that. Truth is, I found that ring right after I first met Marya. Something she said jarred my mind and I remembered using the ring for a bookmark. There it was! Right between the pages. I kept putting off telling Marya, I so enjoyed her *dukkerin*."

Then Aunt Lolly looked deep into my eyes. "And Dearie," she said softly, "Marya left *this* for *you*." She reached into her pocket and brought out a scrap of red cloth! "She said to tell you 'found.'" Aunt Lolly had tears in her eyes as she added, "You know what it means."

I nodded dumbly. I couldn't talk. I was all choked up. Friends forever, my heart was beating out the words over and over. *Best* friends, I thought pressing the scrap to my cheek. One thing I had worried about. I knew Marya was *my* friend, but did she feel the same about me? After all, I was only a *gorgio* — plain — living an ordinary kind of life. Now I knew Marya thought I was someone special. The red amulet was proof!

Aunt Lolly perked up with a deep breath. "She had the gift all right," she said. "I'll miss her. Talking to me of the Gypsy ways, telling me tales told around the fires in the *dingle*. Using the Rom language to speak of the spirits of the wood and wold. It was as if Mama had been here talking to me again."

I knew just how Aunt Lolly felt. I'd miss Marya with all my heart. But I guess I'd known all along that some day she would leave. Marya had been right when she said the spirits were not pleased with my secret wish. It was a wrong wish for Marya. It would have meant that her mama was still in jail. It would have meant that Marya was no longer Gypsy-free the way her life was meant to be.

I hugged Aunt Lolly, and Walter and I told her good-bye. Outside I noticed the leaves in Aunt Lolly's yard were already turning to reds and yellows and oranges — Gypsy colors, I thought feeling a secret sad-happy way.

That afternoon, when our mother drove Walter to his trombone lesson, I carried out my plan. I took

Marya's money and went across Mr. Mortz's pasture to where the haunted house had been.

I stood by the blackened foundation thinking about that first day I met Marya. How she'd propped herself against the sagging front door like she owned the place, with her head thrown back and her black eyes flashing and yelled, "That's right! I'm a Gypsy, a Rom, Tribe of Marks, strain of Kalderasha, seventh daughter of a seventh daughter!"

Marya, who hadn't had a chance to go to school, but who knew more about nature and goodness and the real meaning of things than she could ever have learned in a million schools. Marya, my friend forever.

And I knew then that Marya really could cast spells. She had cast one on me. Because somehow now I didn't mind taking the fourth grade over again — not this one time. I'd learned something besides Gypsy ways from Marya. I'd learned that believing in yourself makes other people like you.

I marked off the seven steps from the foundation. I found the spot easily this time. I pulled out the damp dirt until the jar was uncovered. I picked it up and stuffed Marya's money inside. I put the jar back into the hole. After I'd covered it good with dirt and the clumps of pasture grass, I stood up, looked over toward the woods, and whispered,

"Straw, draw, crow caw.
By my life I give thee law.
Spirit of earth, spirit of sky,
Let this treasure safely lie."

Then I said, *"Dell-o-del"* into the wind, and the wind in the pines at the edge of Mr. Mortz's pasture truly sang the words back to me. I knew then I was a True Rye, because only a Gypsy or a True Rye can hear the music on the wind.

I walked slowly back across the pasture toward home. When I crossed the broken place in the fence I saw High-Pockets throwing his baseball against his roof and catching it. "Come on, *gorgio*," I called out to him. "I've got time to pitch you a few."